IT'S ALWAYS THE LITTLE THINGS

A Keeping Track of Crime Mystery

IT'S ALWAYS THE LITTLE THINGS

A Keeping Track of Crime Mystery

Randy Becker

ABSOLUTELY AMAZING eBOOKS

ABSOLUTELY AMAZING eBOOKS

Published by Whiz Bang LLC, 926 Truman Avenue, Key West, Florida 33040, USA

It's Always the Little Things copyright © 2015, 2017 by Randolph W.B. Becker. Electronic compilation / paperback edition copyright © 2017 by Whiz Bang LLC.

For information contact
Publisher@AbsolutelyAmazingEbooks.com

ISBN-13: 978-1945772498 (Absolutely Amazing Ebooks)
ISBN-10: 1945772492

To Dan MacIntosh, Chef on the Twentieth Century Limited, who taught me some little things essential to this story.

IT'S ALWAYS THE LITTLE THINGS

A Keeping Track of Crime Mystery

1

IT'S ALWAYS THE LITTLE THINGS

Getting ready for a trip, no matter how joyfully anticipated, is always a challenge.

For her, this time, it was not just a challenge but more of a trial.

For him, this time, it was more than a trial, it was a challenge.

Had they known each other it might have meant that the one canceled the other out, or worst case they multiplied each other into either total chaos or complete inertia.

He. He was Alexander P Nottingham. Dr. Alexander P Nottingham. The former Alexandre Notchinsky.

Physics professor at Princeton, Nobel-laureate, world-peace advocate, and one of the few who understood the secrets of string theory.

He began life in Russia, the second son of a not-so-distinguished Soviet Army non-commissioned Officer. His academic acumen and his scientific insights had shown through the rough military conditioning of his upbringing and by the time he was ten he was marked by Soviet scouts for promotion into special educational opportunities for the gifted.

By the age of fifteen he had achieved the status equivalent to most Ph.D.'s in physics in the west but was just coming into his stride. While Russian eyes were turning more and more to the macro – outer space, global power grids, energy resource maximization – his eyes were probing existence and the formulas of existence for the micro and even smaller. He had the intuitive sense that it's always the little things that matter, and that make up matter. Understanding them was the test, using them was merely simplistic application. One of his favorite phrases was "it would be trivial to show" when describing the outcome of some formula. His students always yearned for him to show them, because what was trivial to him was less-than-obvious to almost everyone else.

His rise through the ranks of the scientific elite was not universally regarded as desirable. Many in the oligarchy which was Soviet science thought they detected a slight proclivity toward a universalism that threatened Russian dominance. They knew they must accord him welcome because of his brilliance but that did not mean they must accord him inclusion. He was an outlier.

The Soviet Union was not unlike other great imperialist powers; in its waning days of power and control it tightened the noose on the very life-blood of its intellect in search of an imposed stability. Alexandre was never rounded up for questioning but his parents were. A routine inquiry, it was called, that resulted in a charge against his father for misappropriation of military equipment: 48 rolls of toilet paper. The trial was set but the fall of the Soviet Union intervened.

Alexandre had had enough of the jealous professional bickering, the threats against family, the limitations of thought. At a physics conference in Geneva he walked out of the meeting, into the train station on the Swiss side, through to the platforms that were technically French soil, and began a new life in the west. A few years later he assisted his parents in their relocation to Canada. He wanted them away from the remnants of Soviet mentality and the turmoil in the wake of the demise of the cold war. His older brother, who stayed on in Russia, died of alcoholism a few years ago.

Alexandre was quickly welcomed at Princeton and became America's primary theorist about the sub-atomic, dimensional nature of existence. He was "the man" when it came to String Theory. In a dramatic rebuff to the culture that had nurtured him and then harassed him, he legally changed his name to Alexander P Nottingham (the "P" stood for nothing, only a sop to the endless forms that require an entry for middle initial).

This genius of theory was, however, an apparent total failure at practicality. He could outline the formulae for multiple dimensions but never did seem to figure out how to program his VCR with the remote. He memorized rail timetables but often reported he missed connections in train stations which were unfamiliar. Twice a year he was either an hour early or an hour late for appointments for half a day or so.

Today had been one of those days when all the planning and logic seemed to fail him. Again, it's always the little things. His secretary, Charles, had neatly entered in Alexander's various calendars: leave for conference in Chicago. By leave, everyone at Princeton knew this meant, take the train. Alexander never flew. He never said why.

For some reason, Alexander told people that he would get the dinky over to Princeton Junction and head south to Washington, as he did so often for government meetings. In DC he would change to train number 29, The Capitol Limited, arriving the next morning in Chicago. From Union Station in Chicago he would take a cab across the loop to get what he stilled called an "IC Electric" train south to the University of

Chicago. But he never looked at his tickets.

As he attempted to board the apparently "right" train south at Princeton Junction in the presence of several colleagues, the conductor told him he was boarding the wrong direction. Once again, right theory, wrong practice, or so it would seem. The colleagues silently just nodded at each other as if to say, "Yep, that's how he is."

So over to the northbound side he went, onto the train into New York City, where he would change to train number 49, the Lake Shore Limited. In fact, if anyone really knew him they would know he preferred that route because he knew his small room would be much nicer on the Lake Shore Limited – bigger windows and private rest facilities.

But it also meant navigating New York's Penn Station – that was unfamiliar territory for him. He hated it. Low ceilings, lots of commuter bustle, noise, dirt, ugh. Fortunately a Red Cap on the platform as his train from Princeton Junction pulled in directed him to the Club ACELA lounge, away from the madness that is Penn Station. Comfy lounge chairs, clean bathrooms, some refreshments ... but O, did they have to have endless TV news programs blaring on and on? Always the same, about several smaller world powers causing problems for the United States.

In the hour or so until his train was scheduled to leave, Alexander played a game he had played since childhood. He looked at the others in the lounge and tried to guess who would join him when his train was called. Everyone in the lounge was traveling in some kind of special car: the higher speed ACELA to Washington or Boston, the business class cars to upstate New York, or a sleeping car for places like Atlanta, Miami, or Chicago. So there was a sameness to them all.

But, could he detect some clue about their destination. A pair of gloves, a winter hat, pale skin, a briefcase, an accent. He had whittled the total down to a small circle when the first train was called, and several he had marked as traveling companions had marched off to board. So much for his deductive powers.

He tried again, and his success rate was hovering around 60% when at last train 49 was called. He joined the small throng being gathered to be led down to the sleeping cars. Funny, he didn't recognize one of the people in the group as having been in the lounge earlier, but maybe she had just slipped in at the last moment.

While the bigger bags were taken trainside by the Red Cap on the baggage elevator, the passengers were taken down the long escalator to where the train waited. Stainless steel glistened and red-white-blue striping created a single band across the three sleeping cars.

His was the second car along, 4911, room 1. He liked all the ones in the assignment because ironically few singularities existed in nature. For him, a number 1 or any of its multiples was an invention, a device, a human trick of mind. He contended you could easily fool almost anyone by interjecting unexpected, unnatural elements. They would continue to see the expected, the natural, and literally not see the rest.

One of the reasons he loved riding the train was that he really didn't have to interact with anybody much. Once he had given his ticket for scanning to the conductor and conversed briefly with the car attendant, he could shut and lock his door, close the hall curtains, and be safely and comfortably enclosed in his little cocoon of a room.

He could avoid having to engage in inane

discussion over dinner in the diner by having the attendant bring his meal to the room.

He was content. He was safe. He was on his way. To Chicago, with his attaché case, his winter hat, his gloves, his pale skin, and his accent. It's always the little things that make the difference.

2

BEING INVISIBLE

Her teacher had been her father. He said half of being successful is learning how to be invisible. People who stand out attract problems.

He had worked for decades tending to sleeping cars. First for the Pullman Company, and then for AMTRAK. First as "Boy" or "George," and then as Robert, the car attendant.

Especially in the earlier days, soon after World War II, when his assignments would take him deep below the Mason-Dixon line, he credited much of his survival to being basically invisible.

He had an oft-shared philosophy about invisibility. "You've got your wallflowers, the kind of people who naturally blend into the woodwork. But what trips them up is two things: there's always someone who is going to fall for that look, and in any social setting they stand out as much as they hide away. And then you've got your folk who are actively trying to hide, the sneak thief or the pickpocket. A few of them pull it off, but their success always depends on their being like everyone else in the situation. Put a black man like me down on Peachtree in Atlanta at 5 pm and I couldn't pull it off even during an eclipse. BUT, then you've got the smart ones. They are the ones who do what everyone else is doing, just not so much. They are more like reflections of people than people. Even a reflection has something special about it, but when you try to look again to see that reflection it is gone from sight and memory."

He would then look at her and say "I want you to be one of the smart ones."

Her education on this point was not an easy one. Try being a girl, a black girl, a black girl from a middle-class home, a black girl from a middle-class home with a mind as fine as the best of them, a tall black girl from a middle-class home with a fine mind and a keen sense of justice. Everything about her made her stand out.

For her father, it was OK to be a girl – "half the world are women" he would say. But don't be at one extreme or the other. Dress well, but not too well. Use some makeup if you want, but not too much makeup.

As for being black, her father's advice was the contradiction of his own lived experience: "be proud of who and what you are, but don't wear pride on your sleeve. Black may be the color of your skin, but don't let it also be the color of your soul."

Robert was always sure that it was far better to be middle-class than either too rich or too poor. One always looked wanting and the other always looked needy, both qualities that made it hard to fade away.

He delighted from her earliest days in how quick of thought she was. The fifth child in the household, the baby, the one girl, she was the center of so much attention and at the same time neglected in the demands of the others. She had to make a place for herself that would be appreciated. Her mind was her own, and she developed it as thoroughly as she could.

He would scold her when she used what she knew to obscure what she might observe. "A know-it-all hasn't seen it all, or lived it all, but just act like they have."

And her father would always be quick with a rejoinder, "I may be dumb, but I'm not stupid," whenever she would let her intellect cloud her better moral sense.

Moral sense? That she had in abundance. Her spirit weighed all things on the delicate balance of justice. Was it just that in Kindergarten some children got to go to the water fountain first, while others had to wait, and wait? Was it just when a boy was chosen for the 8th grade graduation speech simply because he was a boy? Was it just that couple tickets to the Prom were $40, but single tickets were $25? Her father would often remind her, "You need to make a choice: always being right or always being effective."

According to what age she was, she found her father's advice to be insulting to her gender, her race, her nascent socialism, her intelligence, and her sense of moral outrage. But by the time she was 21 and graduating *summa cum laude* from university, she had come to find his guidance to have been helpful, extremely helpful.

In any number of occasions she had been able to make herself invisible. Others got carded, but she never did. Others got arrested, but she never did. Others got hit on by undesirable men and women, but she never did. Others got mugged in the area around the university, but she never did.

But there was one thing her father had given her that she wished he had not. Her name. Why any black man named Robert would name a child Lee was beyond her. He said it was a name that added to the invisibility, a name without a gender implication.

It was her last name that was even a bigger problem: Strangler. He was Robert M. Strangler. A slave name, not even an owner's name but the nickname of one who was quick to put away troublesome snakes on the plantation. "Go get Strangler," the overseer would yell, and her ancestor would be summoned to do his thing.

Lee Strangler. Ugh!

She lived with it for all those year growing up, but it seemed like it would be the one big impediment to being invisible. So she tried on a number of identities, different names. In the end she made her choice.

She would remain legally Lee Strangler, but in her professional life she would be Lee Comstock.

And who was Lee Comstock?

On this day she was the recently retired detective for the New York Police Department, assigned for most of her career in Queens.

Upon leaving university, she had considered a legal career but one semester into law school told her it was too much about loopholes and not enough about justice. So, she switched to a program in Criminal Justice, with a specialization in forensics. She excelled in the program but when she attended the 25 year reunion of her class several people seemed surprised that she had been in their class. Ah, she thought, Lee Comstock was invisible.

Of course, she did her time on the beat, at the starting position in the police hierarchy. She soon found she had a knack for getting closer to situations than other police were allowed because people didn't notice her. Some kind of cognitive dissonance: black woman cop?

One of the results of her name was that when she left messages for people, they called her back: saying Lee Comstock needed a call-back seemed to evoke the assumption that a powerful man had called. She was always amused when that call-back would come, she would answer "Comstock" and the caller would say "This is Mike – put him on – I am returning his call."

Through these encounters she learned that just being a little off-balance, feeling a little guilty for making the assumption would mean that the caller would tell her more than perhaps they had originally intended.

As her investigative success grew, her career

developed, leading to the position as the head of homicide investigation, a lavish retirement dinner, and now the regular pension checks rewarding her for 30 years of duty.

Today she was just a civilian, not an ex-cop but a frazzled traveler packing for a trip to San Francisco. A frazzled traveler who had to remember to bring all the identification for Lee Strangler because that was still her legal name.

The AMTRAK tickets would be in that name. The train manifest would be in that name.

Check. She put the ID cards she needed into her wallet.

Check. She had the ticket pdf's on her phone

Check. She had canceled the newspaper and arranged for someone to check on the house.

Check. She had packed everything, twice. But now

Damn. The carryon she had packed developed a leak of lingerie through a broken zipper

Check. Substitute suitcase found and filled.

Check. Taxi called to take her to the Long Island Railroad to travel into Penn Station

Check. It should have been here by now

Check. It really should have been here by now.

Damn. There goes the train

Shit. Now the cabbie shows up

OK. He can take her directly to Penn Station

Damn. Talk about expensive

Check. It is not rush hour yet

Check. Penn Station with 23 minutes to go, not the 90 minutes she had planned

Check. Into Club ACELA just as the boarding call is made

Check. Substitute suitcase wheels negotiate the escalator

Check. She has made it to her car, to her room, to her seat.

Check. The train leaves on time

And through all the prep two pieces of advice she held close merged into a single persona. It had come from two unlikely sources: her father and the long-retired former homicide chief, her predecessor.

Her father from a railroad perspective told her "always travel like it is your first trip, or else you will become someone else's authority." He had plenty of retirement stories about what happened when current sleeping car attendants and even other passengers learned of his long career of service. He was always shocked by how many passengers would ask him to do favors or run errands when he was traveling in retirement. "I may be named Robert, but to some I will always be George."

Captain Lagrese told her (at her retirement dinner), "unless you want to be the cop on the scene, don't be an ex-cop. And by that I mean don't say it, don't act it." He, too, had stories of neighbors and strangers who expected him to still act the policeman for them.

How would this feel, she wondered.

Taking this trip across the country, trying to be invisible so she could be herself, trying to be the novice traveler so she would not be asked to take on someone else's naiveté, trying to be anything other than a cop so the safety of others would not bein her hands.

This would be a trial for her. Could she slip back into the invisible identity of Lee Strangler. One thing she knew for sure, if she wanted that to happen, it would be the little things that would make the difference.

3

CAR 4911, ROOM 2

It had been about half way down the stairs from the taxi unloading zone to the AMTRAK waiting level that Detective Lee Comstock had disappeared and Lee Strangler had appeared. By the time she got to the AMTRAK area she was the novice train rider she wanted to appear to be.

She perfectly well knew where the ClubAcela was, but she asked several people in a sing-song voice. At the door she stood puzzled for a long time as if she didn't know to ring the bell and be buzzed in.

Inside she had fumbled for her train number and her ticket voucher, muttering little self-incriminations of incompetence. She asked twice if she should follow the Usher who was taking people down to the train. She was one of the last in line down the escalator.

At the bottom of the escalator she asked which way her car was, and fumbled again for her ticket voucher to show the Usher so he could direct her.

Here is the secret she knew from the decades of police work: everyone tries to appear competent, even the stupidest of criminals. Bravado, bluff, bravery, bullshit ... all acts to try to hide that a person doesn't know what they are doing. So in a world of facades and fakery, a person who acts like she doesn't know anything is easily dismissed because they pose no threat to anyone. People who know they are making it all up as they go along have their radar fine-tuned for how others are doing the same. The simple act of not seeming to be competent, capable, in control, throws such radar out of whack.

In other words, she became a person everyone would notice but few, if any, would really remember.

Not really remember because she would appear to pose no threat to the fictions of their own lies.

Once into this role, Lee felt more and more comfortable. And so it flowed more easily. It took the poor car attendant three tries to get her pointed in the right direction of her room. Lee loudly asked all the people in the aisle where the smaller rooms were, "Where's Room 2?" As she did, she noted that the door to Room 1 had already been rolled closed and the hallway curtains drawn. What's up with that?

But heads like horizontal gophers poked out into the hallway from other rooms and in a chorus confirmed she was standing in front of it.

"This little bitty room? Where's the bed? Where's the toilet?" elicited a few comments about the Attendant would show her, while others offered only groans.

So into Room 2 she went. As she had on several other trips. There was nothing new for her here. In fact, she had a funny feeling she had been in this same room before – the very car and this very room. When she found the small piece of duct tape with an "LS" written on it keeping the wastebin from rattling, she knew she was right.

She was relieved that she didn't recognize any of the onboard staff – any one of her father's friends or staff from other trips would get in the way of her performance. No, she was allowed to be just another first-time passenger, clueless about nearly everything.

So, she played with everything in the room – turning on and off fans, dropping the sink from its upright locked wall position, lifting the little seat to see the stainless steel potty ("Why, there it is!"), she was a pure AMTRAK novice.

But all the while her cop eyes were looking about, her cop instincts were sensing. Most people were either settling in, or talking across the hallway to others in their groups, or starting their evening libations after a trip to the ice station down the hall ("What, they give us ice? Had I known I would have brought my own stuff.")

But Room 1 was closed, still. She could sense it was occupied and she used an excursion to see where the ice came from as an excuse to see if she could find the manifest for the passengers scheduled on today's train, or at least this car. She couldn't see one out in plain sight.

Instead, she wandered off onto the platform through the next vestibule, trying to look as dazed as possible. The Attendant at that door asked if she could help. "I'm all turned around, I think. I know I am in Room 2, but can't remember which car." The attendant immediately offered to help her, producing a sheaf of folded computer printouts.

"What's your name," the Attendant asked.

"Strangler," Lee replied.

"Strangler?"

"Yes, that's right. O, look there, I see it, in Room 2 in Car 4911. But which one is 4911?"

"That's the one toward the front of the train from here."

"But which way is the front and which way is the rear?"

"OK – see that car there with the two large doors on the side but no windows? That's the baggage car, and it is on the rear.

"O, there, I see it. OK, thanks" Lee said as she tried to enter the rearward car.

"No, M'am. To the front!"

"Oh, that's right."

While all of this had been going on, Lee had shot a quick glance at the manifest that showed her in Room 2 of the 11 car, but then looked up to see that Room 1 was for "Nottingham, Alexander" from New York to Chicago.

Hmmm, that name seemed somehow familiar, but she could not quite place it. That would require some online searching behind her own closed door ... no, wait. She was not on a case, she didn't need to know. She knew that even a little more trying to figure out the guy behind the closed door would begin to jeopardize her own act of not being any kind of railfan and not being an ex-cop. It's always the little things, like getting too interested in something which the character you are playing wouldn't care about.

So, she used her stroll back toward Room 2 as an excuse to say "hi" to folks along the way in her persona of the newbie. On the right was the shower room, closed off now she knew to keep people from using it as a place to store luggage. Opposite it was the Attendant's room – its door was also closed, but the half-drawn curtains revealed the usual Attendant nest of mess.

Rooms 11 and 12 were vacant, awaiting people who would board later. Room 10 had an older couple of ample proportions who took up most of the room by their own presence. They looked like they were ready for a nap.

Room 9 had a woman and a small child, probably about three: the two of them were busily going through bags of toys for some desired object.

Rooms 7 and 8 were a family of four, the two parents and two pre-teen boys. They were speaking what Lee knew was Dutch, but to which she responded, "Sounds like you're not from around here." Their respectable foreign English recounted the story of the start of a great train trip across America. They were

Pier and Mies, and their sons Jacob and Daniël. So, they would all be with her beyond Chicago as well.

Rooms 5 and 6 were also vacant, and her roving eye had been able to see that 5 was for a person named Hildebrandt boarding in Schenectady and leaving the train in Toledo while 6 was for someone named Francis who would board at Utica and ride to Chicago.

Room 4 had a handsome older man, probably in his 70s, who was enjoying both a book and a Scotch. His pleasant smile to her "Hi" was neither encouraging nor dismissive.

Room 3 had been marked on the manifest for someone named Carlisle, New York to Chicago; as of yet it was unoccupied.

And then there was her room and the closed door of Room 1.

She ventured around the bend in the aisle, which put the hallway against the outer wall of the car where the much grander bedrooms were located. As usual, one could detect little about either room except that the occupants were ensconced and the door shut. Bedroom H, the one at that end of the car, closest to the car's entrance vestibule, was reserved for Handicapped passengers, and one was being wheeled into the room just then. The elderly woman looked barely awake, and the equally elderly man who was pushing her looked eager for a chance to sit and rest.

That was it. Ahead of there loomed the not-ready-for-busines-yet-M'am Dining Car, a café car with tables, and then the coaches.

This was Lee's world for the next eighteen hours or so.

She retreated to her Room 2, and settled in. She was pleased to note the train had been assembled the way she hoped it would be, so her Room 2 was on the side of the Hudson River between New York and

Albany. Always a treat to see – but remember, she told herself, you've never seen it before.

Departure was scheduled for 3:40pm. At about 3:35pm, Lee began to hear the sounds of closings. Doors from hallways to vestibules being shut, doors from the platform to the cars being shut. At 3:40 on the nose, with a slight groan akin to the sound that people make when they stand after being seated for a long time, the train came to life and slowly began to move. Just at that moment a mature man, all business and more than a little handsome, came around the bend in the aisle from the front of the train. He looked trim and fit and composed.

"Ah, Yes, Room 3 – almost didn't make it. But did." and with that the presumed Mr. Carlisle arrived into his Roomette, and Lee could hear the sound of the seat being adjusted to recline. About 30 seconds later the Car Attendant appeared toting two carry-on size suitcases.

"Where would you like them, sir?" "O, put the black one up in that damn cubbyhole, and leave the red one down here with me."

"Yes, Sir, excuse me while I climb up ... there, that one is out of the way,"

"Thank you," and Lee thought she heard the shuffling sound of money changing hands.

"Thank you, sir!"

The Attendant, with one hand in his pocket, now appeared in Lee's doorway.

"Is this your first time traveling in this kind of car?"

"How could you tell?"

After a slight pause, the Attendant then began to introduce himself, Bruce, and go over the many elements of the room: air, water, fire (or at least lights and electricity), and earth (or at least sanitation). He explained about how he would make the bed down in the evening, and was on call for any other needs. Lee asked questions about nearly half of what he said.

About mid way through his introduction, the Public Address system buzzed to life and some person somewhere else on the train droned on in a monotone about things like shoes, smoking (don't do it!), food, stops, safety, emergency exits, pesky toilet systems, and....

By the time Bruce was done with his information the announcer had nearly depleted the list of arcane nuances around train travel required by AMTRAK.

But Bruce had one more question for Lee, "If you don't mind saying so, why are you traveling by train?"

Lee Strangler could easily say "I've never done it, and it was kind of on my bucket list, especially after watching some of those old movies."

But Lee Comstock knew there was another, deeper, truer answer. She had been called out too often to the reedy expanses of Jamaica Bay or Flushing Bay to deal with the mangled remains of travelers whose flights ended in tragedy. Too many memories.

"Well, M'am, I hope you find it a good experience. Dining Car person will be along in a little bit to make your dinner reservation."

"O, dinner on a train. I can't wait."

With that a distant chime sounded and Bruce walked toward the bend in aisle, looked up at the annunciator, and then came back toward Lee's room. But instead he turned to Room 1, push the overhead buzzer button for that Room, and said "Yes, sir."

A deep voice with an accent told Bruce that he didn't want a dinner reservation, but that he wanted his dinner brought to the room later – he would tell him when.

"Very good, sir. Just ring, as you did."

The door had not opened a crack; the curtains had not stirred. Only a voice had spoken.

Now, with her act in place, Lee could settle back and enjoy the ride. Soon she was enjoying the kind of afternoon reverie that only a traveler on a sedate mode of travel can know, the afternoon nap. The rocking motion of the train, the sweet memories of trips with her father, and the luxury of having nothing she needed to do.

Beneath her, barely rising to her consciousness, were the slight rumbles of the bridge at Spuyten Duyvil, the slight sway across the interlocking onto the old New York Central main, the whoosh of passing through commuter stations overtaking a local at Yonkers. She figured she would let herself snooze until the Croton-Harmon stop but just south of Ossining and the imposing walls of Sing Sing Prison, a knock at her door roused her from her dreams. It was the dining car person, making reservations for dinner.

She knew the drill all too well: seatings at 5:15, 7:30, and 8:30, and it was advised that New York passengers take the 5:15 because at Albany the people from Boston would board and later seatings would be crowded. Lee dropped back into her novice mode and asked about 6:30, "my usual time to eat at home," only to be told that they would be in the Albany station then and not serving while there. "OK, then, I'll take 5:15," she announced. "Very good, M'am" was the reply.

The dining attendant then turned toward Room 1, and Lee interrupted him, "I heard him tell Bruce he would be taking his dinner in his room, and I think he wants to be left alone." She said it in a way that she hoped the person on the other side of the closed door would hear and know she was watching out for him, or at least watching him.

"I'll talk to Bruce about it," was the response before the man taking the reservations proceeded down the hall to make his repetitive speech about times and menus.

The transaction had taken only a few minutes but

it was enough to completely stir Lee from her sleepy state. She turned her attention to both the passing landscape of the Hudson Valley and the Kindle book she was reading. The landscape won out. The river was always so interesting ... odd footbridges over the railroad leading to stairs down to nowhere ... the once busy waterfronts now converted to upscale housing and dining ... Peekskill and its sharp curve around which Eva Marie Saint had flirted with Cary Grant as they traveled north by northwest ... the graceful Bear Mountain Bridge ... West Point on the other shore ... the old ferry dock at Beacon ... the high bridge over the Hudson at Poughkeepsie. Familiar territory that grounded her even as she remembered to exclaim about it all periodically like a new found treasure.

She was thinking about the pace of progress: it was not all that long ago that a steamboat made history on this very river, and then the railroad came, and then the Interstate Highways whose bridges superseded the ferries, and finally the airplanes which demoted this train, her train, to history even as she experienced it as comfort.

The intercom crackled, and a disembodied voice issued the first call for those with 5:15 dinner reservations. Of course, she was all the way back by Bruce's little Attendant's room before he sent her in the other direction toward the diner.

Almost all of the traffic into the diner came from the sleepers because all sleeping car passengers had their meals included in the price of their rooms. A few coach passengers who savored more than microwave pizza and zapped burgers came from the other direction. In the middle of the car, the Lead Attendant, the one who had taken reservations was working like a traffic cop, directing people to seats.

"No, if you are a two-some you have to sit next to each other. Others will need to be seated with you."

"How many?"

"Sit right there with those folks."

Railroad dining cars are both a delight and a challenge, depending on whether you function as an extrovert or an introvert. Passengers are seated four to a table, filling one table before another is opened for occupancy. Quick conversations or deafening silences can be the result.

Lee was relieved to find herself being seated at the window, facing forward, river side, about 4 tables in ... best seat in the house! Being seated alongside her was a woman who appeared to be in her 20s, from the coaches. She was surprised because younger people rarely took advantage of the dining cars unless they were in the sleepers. Then two men slid opposite them – it was the older man from Room 4 and the late arrival in Room 3.

Room 4, seemingly well loosened from his Scotch, set about making the introductions. Farrell, Robert Farrell, "Uncle" Bob Farrell, from Menomonee Falls, Wisconsin. (This would be easy to remember because no one ever called her father "Bob." He was Robert all the time!) Retired teacher, shop-teacher, just heading home from his granddaughter's wedding on Long Island.

Next up was Room 3, Clayton Carlisle, or CC as he liked to be called. Artistic director for a company that provides support for trade shows. "One wound up in Parsippany and the next one is on for out by O'Hare airport."

Lee decided to go next. "Lee Strangler. So, if any of you need a strangler tonight, you know where to find her." (Giggle). "If any of you know any secrets of this train traveling, I would sure appreciate any advice. I am going all the way to the other coast, figuring if I was going for a hundred miles I ought to go the whole three thousand."

Uncle Bob immediately suggested Scotch was the best advice he could give. Didn't need a mixer, could go neat with a little water or on the rocks.

CC just smiled and said he would get back to her if he thought of anything.

Jean Steele, on her way to a job interview in Syracuse, was the coach passenger. "This is not my first train trip, but almost all of it has been out of New York on the, what do they call it, the Corridor. When I heard I could get to Syracuse on a real train, one with sleepers and a diner, I just had to try it."

And so the meal progressed ... recommendations made, diets considered (Jean was Vegetarian), beverages ordered, and the scenery flew by. The food all arrived at the same time so no one was left sitting waiting. Lee always loved the steak she would get on AMTRAK, but tonight she had to make a big deal about a steak actually cooked at 70 miles per hour.

They became a jovial group, all interested in talking about the train, recent news events, and the panorama outside their window. Too soon the dessert and coffee was being brought. Lee knew they were nearing the point where the freight tracks diverted to a vast yard south of Albany while the passenger tracks followed the river. From here on the speed increased greatly, above 100 miles per hour, which would become a great test for the 60+ year-old Diner. One did not need a speedometer to sense the acceleration – the random rattles and shakes did it for one. Before long, coffee was sloshing in every cup. Lee instinctively put her spoon in her cup with the bowl of the spoon down, not up, immediately quelling the tsunami of coffee that threatened the tablecloth. Uncle Bob noticed and did the same thing, adding, "Neat trick there, Strangler."

The dining car crew was cleaning around them to prepare for arriving in Albany, loss of the main lighting for a few minutes, and then the predicted groundswell of Bostonians.

The party broke up with CC suggesting that Lee should leave a few dollars for a tip even though the meal was free. "They will remember you in the morning if you do, I can tell you." Of course Lee knew this, but acted like it was all new to her.

Lee and CC headed back toward the sleepers once Lee had gotten CC to lead the way. Uncle Bob and Jean went forward, Jean toward the coaches and Uncle Bob "to check out the supplies in the Club Car."

The Albany Station is not in Albany, but across the river from it. Built at the location of an older station from the bankrupt days of PennCentral, the platforms were undergoing major upgrading to match the more modern station itself. Lee planned to get off for some fresh air but Bruce seemed worried about her doing so. "Good," she thought, "he's falling for my incompetence act."

"Now, don't go too far away from the platform ... and even if the train moves prior to 7pm, just keep an eye out for this car – I've put that red card in the aisle window by the vestibule so you'll know it's your car. OK?"

Lee snapped a cute little salute, "Yes, sir!"

What she had had time to do before stepping off the train was to sniff. A quick sniff outside Room 1 – smelled like he had been brought a steak dinner. Outside Room 4 she paused and sniffed and was surprised that she could detect no odor of Scotch. Just then CC rolled back his door and asked if she was off to the platform as well. "Lead the way," Lee had said, and so CC was the gallant guide to the front of the car.

Bruce called out "Mind the gap" as the train ground to a halt.

Lee was a little miffed. She had hoped they would

come in on the westside of the platform. That way she could have gotten a look inside Room 1 from the platform. Now it was going to be a little more difficult. Wait, why was she still following up on this mystery, or was it even a mystery? Mind your own business, Lee. Not everything that seems suspicious is suspicious.

It was probably best that she convince herself of this because any other vantage point of Room 1 was well behind security fencing of the renovation projects.

The Boston cars were added to the train, through baggage was shifted to a single baggage car, cigarette smokers fed their addiction in hasty puffs on as many cigarettes as they could manage, and then the final boarding call was made. As always, Lee could tell who on the platform was from the New York section, and who was from the Boston section. The New Yorkers looked business-like ... a short trip up the river. The Bostonians looked like exiles, a trip over the mountains taking them into a land beyond culture. For several of the older folk from Boston, having to wait until 7:30pm for dinner left them looking fatigued and annoyed.

7:05pm, departure time, came and went, and it was about 7:12pm as they finally departed, the delay becoming evident as another train from the west slid by them as they headed west.

By then it was dark, and the wonders of the Mohawk Valley would be lost to sight. But for Lee, the best part of the day was just coming. She pushed the call button for the attendant, and Bruce was there.

"Yes, m'am."

"I think I would like to lie down."

"Just give me a minute, and I will make your bed down. You can sit in Room 6 while I do it."

Lee wandered down the hall to Room 6, noting that Uncle Bob was missing in action. CC had closed his door but she could hear him plugging away on a computer keyboard inside.

In about 5 minutes Bruce was back to get her. "All set – do you want a wake-up call in the morning?"

"Why, do I need one?"

"Not really, unless you plan to sleep until past 9am."

"No, I'm an early riser. Thanks."

Lee noticed that Bruce had a tray of empty dishes in his hand, and from the remains of a steak that were visible she surmised Room 1 had used her room makeup as a time to get rid of the dinner dishes. As she pivoted into her room, she saw the door to Room 1 was again firmly closed and the curtains pulled.

In her own room, Lee did the same. Closed and locked the door, pulled the curtains, changed into her sweats, used the toilet, did a simple evening cleanup, and then snuggled down into bed. Turning off the bright lights and even the blue ceiling nightlight, she pulled back the curtains to the outside window and there it was ... the whole world rushing by in the velvet light of twilight becoming night. Her room darkened as much as she could make it (she stuffed a pillow into the gap below the door where light crept in) meant the world outside seemed lighted.

It was lighted at close range by light coming from the train itself. At a more distant range, it was illuminated by houselights and headlights and streetlights. Overall, it was draped in the pale lunar whiteness of a moon rising toward full.

Also, now freed of the restrictions of the line along the river, the many grade crossings meant the wonderful sound of the horns on the engine signaling their warnings for all. Slight curves meant a glance ahead to see signals of red and green, green for her track. Periodically a sudden light, an approaching roar, and a freight in the opposite direction would roar by.

At one point the train slowed slightly and then she felt the slight sideways motion of being switched to the other track, and as that happened the edge of her hallway curtain flapped for just a moment at its velcroed seam along the door, and at the same moment the curtain edge by the sink in Room 1 also rippled, and she caught a glance of the man in Room 1, not his face but his hand, a toothbrush, and his teeth as he applied the brush to them. Then the two curtains fell back in place, a momentary glimpse into forbidden territory.

Somehow seeing him brush his teeth was comforting to her. A piece of a personal ritual, a reality, part of a process toward sleep. She hoped that he had flossed as much as she had because she suspected the steak had been imbedded in his gums as much as it had been in hers.

Just about then she heard a large bump against her door, and Uncle Bob's voice, thoroughly sing-song, apologized to parties seen perhaps only by Uncle Bob. A slight waft of Scotch followed.

Knowing that the cradle-like motion of the train, her long day, the melatonin she had taken, and her feeling of total at-homeness meant sleep would be coming soon, she put in her earplugs, nestled all the pillows, drew the window curtains closed, and drifted off to sleep.

Utica, Syracuse, Rochester, Buffalo, Erie, Cleveland, Elyria, Sandusky, Toledo all passed as she slept. She would not awaken until the dew was on the grass and the sun rising on Indiana.

4

CHICAGO

Somewhere in eastern Indiana, Lee awoke in that lazy fashion which marks train travel. Through her earplugs she heard the first announcements made in hours: a reminder that the diner was open for breakfast and then the station stop announcement for Waterloo. Since she knew there must have been earlier announcements for Bryan, Ohio, and the first PA announcement from the diner for breakfast somewhere around 7am, she knew had been sleeping soundly.

There are two kinds of people in mornings on trains. Some awaken, dash about as if time were finite and leaking away. Others arose, letting the day in slowly, as if time were elastic and going on forever. As Lee opened her outside curtains an inch at a time so the flooding light would be more welcomed than assaulting, she knew she was an elastic time kind of person. This was not her usual mode. Too many years responding to alarm clocks, roll calls, emergency beepers replaced finally by emergency texts all of which required sudden response had now dissolved into a slower mode of life. It had not immediately upon her retirement, but this transcontinental train trip was, in part, an attempt to re-start the timely timelessness that she had known long ago.

Parts of body stretched, earplugs removed, curtain opened wider, more stretching, sitting up, making her way onto the commode, all the while watching the world outside come to life as well. At several crossings, heralded by the insistent train horn, she saw school buses on their rounds rounding up students. The little towns created and now bisected by the railroad offered up coffee shops lined by cars with dew on their rear windows.

There is a peace in such a morning. No place to go, nothing to do other than live. She felt whole, relaxed, refreshed in a way that she had not felt for a long, long time.

That feeling was accentuated by a wonderful hot shower down the hall in the shower room. The deluxe rooms had their own combined toilet and shower rooms, but the Roomette crowd all shared a single, larger, dedicated shower at the end of the car. Lee was always amazed that so few other travelers used the shower and were amazed when she said she did. She found the luxury of a steamy shower at 79 mph a delight.

The shower washed away whatever lingering layer of the past she carried with her from New York. She had bought a new shower gel for the trip, "Revitalized Morn," which lived up to its name.

Back to Room 2, door closed and locked again, curtains closed again, but a little less carefully than the first night out, and she dropped the robe used for hallway modesty and got dressed for the day. As she did, she looked through a small crack in the curtain across to Room 1 where she was rewarded with another glimpse into the sealed chamber. He was just completing brushing his teeth and now, yes, he was lathering for a shave. My God, she thought, he is using an actual brush and soap, just like Daddy did. Nothing aerosol about him. His hygiene which had comforted her last night now somewhat excited her. This mysterious man of mystery was taking on all kinds of qualities of character.

Lee completed dressing, untangled and brushed her hair, put on a little makeup and lipstick, and felt ready for the day. In the small wall mirror, if she stood as far back as possible, she could see most of herself (she would have to surmise about the shoes) and she liked what she saw. Strong but not harsh, black hair with a few strands of grey falling just above shoulder length without bangs, the twinkle of her dangling amethyst earrings, brown eyes under (well groomed) delicate brows, a nose that had had no fixing and needed none, teeth in good order, full lips a shade of morning sunrise, and a chin that told of heritage from West Africa in a long distant past. Below her 5 foot, 9 inch body was well-proportioned with no hint of gravity's grab. She worked out most days, and would later today in her walk around Chicago's Loop, and it showed (or actually more accurately nothing showed which meant it was all successful).

She pulled open the hall curtains, rolled back the door, and stepped into the hallway. Bruce was coming up the aisle just then and an almost whistle parted his lips. Ah, she thought, I look as good as I think I do.

That positive sense emboldened her. She hesitated just a moment, and then knocked on Room 1's door – "How about some breakfast?"

"I'm good," was a deep, accented, muffled answered.

And so off she went to breakfast, making sure to turn first toward Rooms 3 and 4 before Bruce pointed her in the right direction.

As Lee walked along the corridor toward the diner, she suddenly had a flashback of her mother. She looked so much like her. Like her mother, she was a woman for whom heads turned. She was courted by all the "hot" young blacks in the neighbor, and even beyond. Momma possessed both a gracious beauty and, for her time, a great addition. She had a college degree. She had gone to Hampton Institute, one of the historic black colleges. She was educated and might have been able to write her own ticket. Or her own ticket in the Negro community. Momma always said the problem with an education is that you begin to see horizons not available to everyone. Her dreams went beyond the Negro community but in her time that would not be an option. So instead of fame and fortune, she decided on happiness. Happiness was Daddy.

Lee's mother had been a homebody. She tended all those kids and kept the home fires burning while Daddy had been paying the bills and working across the country. One thing Lee knew for sure, Daddy might have been a traveling man (so to speak) but he never strayed. Momma, so often alone, was a true heart. Theirs was one of those epic lifelong love affairs. She had always felt blessed as a child knowing how solid their family was.

As Lee, and Momma in a sense, walked toward the diner, a heritage of both education and beauty and grace walked with her.

Daddy had told her about the strange relationship between travelers of color and the servants of color on the railroads of America. In his day, he was taught that in the North to look all travelers in the eye and concentrate on business. In the South, one looked at the carpet and concentrated on service.

But with travelers of color in the sleeping cars, most of whom were in the North, one was allowed to relax a bit, to look at the whole person, to appreciate the handsomeness and the beauty of people who looked like one.

The Civil Rights movement of the 1960's had opened transportation to all, and many barriers dropped. With the dropping of barriers came a sameness to the treatment of passengers. But, in an almost instinctual way, AMTRAK staff of color remembered the right of appreciation of passengers of color. Nothing overt, but very subtle. But there none the less.

As Lee strode to the diner, she was aware that the conductor who met her at the vestibule and the waiter who assisted her to her seat in the diner all paused, just for an almost imperceptible moment, to stop working and appreciate. It made her feel very good about herself.

A diner in the morning carries with it an aroma that is like no other. Back when the diner's stoves were fired with Presto-logs or charcoal, it was enhanced by a smokiness unlike any other. Now with electrical griddles, the smell of bacon and sausage coupled with the sweetness of syrups and the butteriness of eggs blends with the strong arousal of coffee to greet the traveler. Ah, I thought I was awake, but now I am truly awake it says.

Lee was seated alone at a table this time ... breakfast is less regimented than dinner. It was the first table along on the right, now north facing, right over the wheels, not her favorite because of its bounciness but on such a morning as this it was delightful. She thought she would breakfast alone until she heard and smelled: CC and Uncle Bob arrived together and seeing her dining alone pointed in unison to the waiter at the empty seats at her table.

On the one hand, Lee was annoyed because she was savoring the alone time. But on the other hand, she was flattered that these two wanted more time with her.

CC looked a little worse for wear and he confessed he had not slept all that well. Uncle Bob, as if on cue, suggested that a proper amount of Scotch would have paved the way for a full night's sleep. Uncle Bob claimed as long a sleep as Lee's. CC only groaned and pointed to his empty coffee cup, which was promptly filled.

Over the next hour, in the start and stop reality of the railroad approach toward Chicago, even as watches lied that no time at all was spent on breakfast because of the time zone change, conversation flowed and Lee Strangler oohed and aahed at many supposedly-newly-encountered things. Lee enjoyed the Railroad French Toast with bacon, Uncle Bob did in scrambled eggs with sausage, while CC managed only the simplest oatmeal and some fruit. Coffee cups were filled often and laughter erupted equally often. Lee noticed how attentive the staff was and decided the advice from the night before about tipping had been on target.

Finally clear of some of the freight interference, which had interrupted a steady flow toward Chicago, the Lake Shore Limited returned to speed, which meant that the coffee danced in their cups. Uncle Bob, placing his spoon upside down in his cup, announced, "See, you can teach old dogs new tricks." He was well pleased with himself. Lee was pleased for him too, marveling that he could remember that much from last evening.

By the second "any thing more for any of you?" the group got the hint and rose to leave. Lee was not surprised to see Uncle Bob head forward, mumbling something about hair of the dog. CC accompanied Lee back toward their sleepers, opening doors for her including the sleeper door, which needed only a push of the button.

As they approached the bend in the corridor, CC whispered to Lee "what do you make of the gent in 1?"

"Not much. Sort of a recluse, I guess, or a celebrity."

"Whatever."

And with that CC headed to his room while Lee ducked into her chamber.

The approach to Chicago is a mixed lot. There is the gradual gathering of humanity out of the agrarian flatlands of Indiana, dotted with the sandy dunes below Lake Michigan. Railroad lines converge, the last interurban railroad in America comes alongside. Suddenly remnants of outdated industry such as open hearth foundries decline amidst the new construction of modern technologies. Once great cities rot into oblivion traversed by interstate highways. Oil is refined. The great Great Lake is glimpsed. Drawbridges and lift bridges cross canals of dark, oily water. Neglected rails of forgotten railroads known by fallen flags of another era crisscross each other.

And then you can see it – the Willis Tower that everyone calls the Sears Tower. Gradually growing around its base buildings that would be big in other settings rise up. Neighborhoods from the turn of another century crowd perfectly symmetrical streets and avenues. More Interstates. Lots of concrete.

Frantic travelers packing up their many things. Announcements about stops, red caps, looking for all your things. Wait for the announcement from your car attendant to leave your seat or room. A brief thank you for traveling AMTRAK. "CHICAGO, Chicago Union Station, CHICAGO."

As the travelers began to pour out of their rooms, Lee held out a last minute hope to see the man in Room 1. Just as she emerged, Uncle Bob called from down the corridor, "Lee, all the best to you – if you ever get to Milwaukee, look me up."

"Thanks Bob," she replied, and seeing CC popping into a gap of exiting passengers, she added, "CC - be well." CC waved to her, and added "It has been a pleasure." She gave him a slight salute in response.

She would regret that exercise in etiquette.

As she turned her head back to the corridor she saw that the curtains on Room 1 were parted, the room empty, the man now just a back taking the corner to the aisle by the deluxe rooms. If she hurried, she might catch sight of him, but CC was now just about to her room, and with a gallant gesture offered her the right of way.

"Kind sir. Thank you."

By the time she was on the platform she could not even identify the back of the man from across the hall. The crowd which swelled as they walked forward made it all the more difficult. Well, that would have to be a story for another day.

One would think that arrival in a town that railroads made would be exquisite, but Lee knew it would be mundane. The train shed had lost the battle with maintenance needs, there was a long walk from the rear of the train to the main station, and that main station was a mere shadow of what was once there. But then, she remembered she had left from perhaps the world's greatest travesty of railroad stations. New York's Penn Station had once been a world-class monument in the manner of Roman baths, demolished to make way for a sports arena. Chicago, not to be outdone and live up to its Second City moniker, had torn down its equally grand and welcoming main arrival and departure area to make way for a commodity trading deck.

In fact, as Lee walked down the platform, she had two distinct perceptions. One was of being part of a great traveling hoard arriving in the city of broad shoulders, full of grit and grace, of frontier and finery. She remembered that scene from Hitchcock of arriving at LaSalle Street Station, the 20th Century Limited having brought a whole cast of characters to sort themselves through murder and international intrigue. Hitchcock, the master, properly brought his train into the unimpressive station of its actual arrival. Chicago, above all else, was a city of reality.

She also had an impression of entering into a burrow. From the high ceilings of the train shed the walkway led up to an entry into a low-ceilinged warren of roped-off areas, narrow hallways leading who knew where.

Lee knew where, and following her memory she wove past semi-hidden escalators upward to somewhere, around newsstands and ticket lines, until she passed through a wide portal into the vast great waiting room of what remained of the real Union Station. Movies had been filmed here. Millions of people, from war, from jobs, from college, fleeing home, fleeing poverty, fleeing the Midwest, had walked through this space. It has the power to take one's breath away, or in Lee's case to give her her breath back. She had felt claustrophobic in the cellar-like modern area of the station, but here … here … the little hairs on the back of her neck suddenly stood on alert, a feeling she had known all too often in her career. She wheeled around but spotted nothing and no one who should be creating that experience. Maybe it was just ghosts from some other time.

Lee went back through the wide portal, back into the maze of passages in search of the baggage storage room. She knew that with her sleeper car ticket for later in the day her bag could be stored and she would be free to get out into the city.

But which city to get out into? Chicago, home of the squealing elevated? Chicago, home of the most diverse architecture in America? Chicago, home of one of the largest collection of museum in the world? Chicago, home to the back-flowing Chicago River? Chicago, home of deep-dish pizza, hot dogs with dayglo relish, and ethnic delights beyond measure?

Lee had about 4 hours to spend, thanks to the on-time arrival of her train; she knew that was a good sign because such performance is rare. But what she did surprised even her. She started walking eastward from Union Station, crossing over the River, under the El, past many restaurants, beyond the Art Institute and Millennium Park, until she could see the expanse of Lake Michigan, and there in a pleasantly mild midday she sat.

She sat gazing across the horizon of water and its endless invitation to peace and contemplation. She sat for over an hour and then slowly she pivoted around and gazed at the dynamic skyline of the city and its provocative invitation to wonder and awe. Sometimes when she was on duty along the Queens waterfront other officers would catch her looking either at the East River or the cityscape of Manhattan with comments about nature and creativity. Long ago she had learned to quiet such thoughts while she was on the job, but here, now, away from the job, she heard those thoughts arising again. A little glimpse of her own rebirth – sometimes you have to retire in order to work things out.

It was all so wonderful, especially her sense that she, in this anonymous city, she didn't need to play the role of Lee Comstock the cop, nor of Lee Strangler, naive traveler. She could just be Lee, whoever Lee was becoming.

She finally let the city release its hold on her, and she began her trip back across the Loop to where another train would be waiting to take her to the West Coast. She made it a grazing trip, food provided by a wide diversity of street food vendors.

But, it was odd. On two different occasions as she stopped to choose, buy, and eat some delicious item, those hairs on the back of her neck alerted her. Something or someone had her intuitions on edge. But neither time was there any seeming reason. Maybe she was just losing it.

She treated herself to re-entry into Union Station

by coming down one of the grand staircases into the Great Hall, an entry that stops nearly everyone mid-flight by the grandeur and immensity of the space and energy of travelers. She let out a long sigh, and found that she could catch her breath more fully than she had in a long, long time. Ahhhh.

But, time and tide and trains wait for none. Retrieve her suitcase. Check into the Metropolitan Lounge in the same manner she had the Club Acela in New York, almost simultaneous with the boarding announcement for Train 5, the California Zephyr.

Time to become Lee Strangler again, novice traveler.

She followed the crowd out to the waiting train, this time made up of the impressive two-story Superliners. She was in Car 511, Room 4. Good, that meant she was upstairs where the noise was less and views were better.

In the process of boarding she spotted the Dutch family, heading for a different sleeper and she waved. Otherwise, no one else seemed familiar to her from the previous train, but of course she had not seen many of the coach passengers.

Departure on any train is very similar. Rooms to be found, introductions of room details to be made, tickets to be scanned, PA announcements about sundry safety regulations, and further announcements about snacks and dinner. Lee barely paid any attention to any of the announcements. She was ready for the next leg of her trip. This one would be more than two full days, and who knew what it might bring.

She found herself once more thinking about the man back in Room 1. She also was thinking about why she was thinking about him. "Lee," she said to herself, "if you get to the point that you are thinking about why you are thinking about why you are thinking about him, maybe Uncle Bob's Scotch would be a good idea." The slight jolt of the train's start broke her train of thought.

Soon they were racing west out of Chicago, passing through the many western suburbs until the old roundhouse at Aurora, now converted to a brewpub, marked the end of the commuter territory, and the train left the last outpost of the east behind.

5

While Lee was in the midst of the trip, the two days from Chicago to California had seemed expansive. There were ample opportunities for naps, viewing from the Sightseer Lounge with its roof windows, spirited discussions over meals, and more scenery than a travel brochure could describe.

Later, when she would try to recall that portion of the trip, she found herself with a mental highlights reel more than a full travelogue. Something seemed to be engaging her mind even while she was experiencing the Rockies and the Sierras at close range. Maybe it was the unfamiliar altitude. Maybe it was the opposite of jetlag, in which the slowing down of time and obligations befuddled the brain. Maybe it was a premonition of what retirement would be like with no need for acute awareness ever again. Whatever it was, it puzzled her but did not seem to trouble her.

She remembered conversations in the Sightseer car with the Pier and Mies and their family. Lee was trying to teach them some of the idioms of American English, and she was joined in the effort by a number of Californians who wanted to add in their own West Coast phrases. Some of it was an education for Lee as well.

With the Dutch family, she felt she could relax a bit. Not disclose much, but she didn't need to do the full Lee Strangler, helpless traveler, role. She had dealt with many tourists from Europe while on duty in Queens, and she knew their culture would restrain them for asking the kind of personal questions that Americans seemed to love. They wouldn't ask about what she did, for instance. That was her business, to them, and only if she offered such information could they ask. She didn't offer, they didn't ask.

For some, the end of a "god-damn long train trip" is welcomed. For others, the end is almost dreaded as the luxury of being cared for without obligation of time or work winds down. Lee felt that sense of longing for the trip to continue even longer. For the first time in years she felt like she had really relaxed, really let her guard down, really just took what came.

But when the train slowly pulled into its last stop in Emeryville, across the bay from San Francisco, she was surprised how that relaxed feeling stayed with her as she transferred to the AMTRAK bus connection into San Francisco.

There were some goodbyes, especially with the Dutch family, the only people who seemed to have made the whole trip with her from coast to coast. But she like most people just ambled over to put her bag under the bus and take a window seat on the bus.

Just about when the bus went into the tunnel midway across the Bay Bridge, when she could not see the beauty of the Bay, the Golden Gate, or the hilly terrain of San Francisco for a moment, she had a moment of trepidation, like she was seeing all these new things but she was forgetting something old, something important.

Just then her cell phone rang. It was a San Francisco number. She almost answered but then hesitated. Who in San Francisco had her number? She hadn't given it to anyone. Was it the owner of the house where her AirBnB was located? No, she had an Oakland number, if Lee remembered correctly. There was no voicemail. But strange that someone in San Francisco would be calling her personal cell phone with its Queens number.

"Clang, Clang" and she was in heaven. The cable cars were all she had ever dreamed of. She rode every line more than once, as often as she could, often going beyond her destination just for the open-air thrill of hanging on. Doubling back to her intended stopping place felt like a bonus, not a burden.

And then there were the F line restored trolleys. From all over the United States and the world, classic examples of how comfortable public transit was in another era.

She was having a tourist's best time.

However, as a tourist, she had placed herself right in the middle of controversy. For her extended stay an AirBnb private apartment in a home made more economic sense than a hotel. Willing to live in a little tougher neighborhood than many tourists might desire, the upper floor in a house in The Mission seemed a great option. She had figured on a few, potentially bothersome people on the streets, especially at night; she had not figured on a few downright unfriendly neighbors upset with her presence in what they deemed an illegal quasi-hotel room in THEIR neighborhood. Didn't matter that just down the street the legal hotel had by-the-hour rates.

Her small suite of rooms, probably originally for either an in-law or some domestic help, had its own entrance. In the morning she would find that the entrance had become an intentional depository of garbage. No, not bags of garbage – the locals were too ecological for plastic bags. Simply garbage of the "let's put this in the compost pile" variety. Oozy, smelly stuff. Not the way she wanted to start her day.

This then explained the broom and dustpan hiding behind the door. She wasn't the first to experience this neighborhood welcome apparently. She looked around for some form of take-away container – a paper bag, a carton, a box – that could be used to contain the removed items. She was rewarded with it being a recycling day and she discovered ample supplies for this necessity lining the curbs of her block.

Then the third morning she noticed the pile came with its own special ornament: a dead rat. Dead from some unknown overdose of filth? A remnant of some other place's demise? A victim of the garbage underneath itself?

She was about to treat *la Rata* to an anonymous sweeping into an IKEA box when she noticed something. The rat had a small piece of wire around its neck ... a twisted, a tightened piece of wire ... the rat had been strangled. Caught, strangled, and placed here on her doorstep. But why?

A convenient disposal, a general warning to interlopers, a generic message about Airbnb, or a more specific message to Lee, Lee Strangler?

While it was easy to push the rat and the other filth into the small box and drop it in the trash receptacle on the corner, it was far from easy to push its memory from her thoughts. It brought her back to her detective mode. It brought her back to worrying about the significance of things. It brought her back to a career-long questioning mode: was she seeing too much or too little in the situation?

However, as the morning fog burned off into a delightful day, her plans for a trip by ferry to Sausalito pressed their way to the front of her mind. The fresh air of the trip, the vistas of the Bay, the waterside seafood for lunch, a walk among the simple and the palatial boats in the marinas, and a sunset ferry return to the city made it a nearly perfect day. Nearly. It was just as she was watching the sun dipping behind the Golden

Gate, turning it into its namesake, that Lee felt it again.

Those hairs on the back of her neck. But this time she recognized it for what it had usually meant. Not necessarily danger. Simply that someone was watching her, observing her. She was the target of someone's attention.

Steeling herself to gain the attitude of nonchalance that had served her well in police duty when she felt the same way, Lee kept her face pointed toward the sunset but behind her sunglasses her eyes were roaming. No, it was not someone right beside her. Now, how to look elsewhere without seeming to look.

Boats can be accomplices in the work of the devious. Just as Lee would have loved to have turned around to scan the others on board, the ferry blew two long blasts on the horn to alert a seemingly oblivious sailboat of its approach. Many on the deck turned at the sound of the horn and Lee saw her chance to look back at the crowd. Most of the others' heads were turned aft toward the wheelhouse, like hers, but in the gangway she thought she saw someone turn away just as she glanced that way. She wasn't sure. Again, the police instinct told her that either the person was acting strangely or the person had some mental disorder, for there was something about their affect that was out of kilter.

Lee told herself it was probably nothing, just the old wary and weary nerves upset with being given so long a holiday. However, better safe than sorry. With that in mind Lee slowly made her way toward the deck where they would disembark, wanting to be toward the front of the crowd. This was her plan – to get off as quickly as possible, move right along to some place of obscurity, and then watch everyone getting off the ferry from that hidden perspective.

More horns, ropes tossed and tied off, rails opened,

gangplank deployed, security chains dropped, and she was the third person onto the Ferry Terminal pier, moving quickly toward the doors into the Main Terminal building. There she dove quickly into the first food shop inside and reversed direction until she was looking back out the rear windows as the dispersing ferry crowd. She knew, from her own approach to the building that the glare on the windows obscured those inside from being seen from outside.

First in a torrent, then in a trickle, they came through the Ferry dock area. No one looked even vaguely familiar. She had just about given up hope of seeing anyone like the fleeting image seen on board. Then among the stragglers someone familiar appears for a second hugging the far side of the walkway, dropping away too soon to leave by walking around the Ferry Building instead of through it. Head down, face away from view, avoiding the route that most people had and would take.

Lee stepped quickly from her place by the windows, exited the shop, pushed her way through the food court area, and out onto the Embarcadero. She thought she had made good time and surely would have been ahead of the slowly moving figure. No, he was now crossing the Embarcadero, dodging around one of the old Milan trolleys, heading into the city. Up Market Street.

Lee followed in her well-trained, discreet way, hanging back just to the point that she was part of the sidewalk crowd but able to see where her subject was headed. A quick right on California, by the end of the cable car line she knew only too well. He was moving along quickly now, turning off California onto Montgomery and then Clay. He was beginning to lengthen the distance between them, and she had to be more careful because there were far fewer people on the streets.

And then he turned into Portsmouth Square Plaza and by the time she reached the entrance by the playground he was gone. Lee stopped and scanned the whole area but could see no one much moving and no one just staying put who resembled her query. She waited a few minutes, moving to stand closer to the trees by the entry way, knowing that sometimes the successful pursuit requires not pursuing but waiting for the bird to be flushed from its cover. Ten minutes later, Lee decided no one was going to show their presence.

She had to admit that the action had been enlivening. She had enjoyed the chase. But maybe it was all just coincidence, all just mistaken assumptions. Maybe her mind, a little angry at being put out to pasture, had conjured it all up.

Lee relaxed. She took several deep breaths. Looked up and saw the few stars visible in town. Then turning around, she headed back along the path she had taken, back toward Market Street and a BART ride back to her house.

Walking the familiar route from BART to her apartment, she wondered what filth she might find in her entry this evening. As she fumbled for her key in her pocket and turned toward her door, carefully scanning for any garbage, her mind registered a pair of shoes too late to avoid the blow on the back of her neck. She instantly saw more stars than anyone should see in town.

She awoke lying like too many denizens of the Mission, crumpled in an entry way, looking the worse for life and wear. Ouch, her head hurt, and her neck was way too stiff. Her whole body felt bruised, the kind of bruised feeling one gets from sleeping in a cramped position. She wondered why no one had bothered to see if she were OK. Why didn't someone call an ambulance, or the police, or both. Or at least try to see if she were dead. Then she smelled herself. She reeked. Or at least where she lay reeked. Slowly getting to her feet she could see the rotting refuse that had been in the doorway, produce well past its prime. But even as she stepped away from the doorway, part of the stench went with her. It must be her coat. She took it off and hung it on the doorknob, and tried walking away again. Some odor, some strong odor lingered. The smell of alcohol. Someone had dumped alcohol on her to make her look like just another smelly drunk.

She smelled like a street drunk. Or, wait, did she? She sniffed again. No rockgut created this aroma – Scotch!

6

THE MORNING AFTER

Fortunately for Lee, her apartment came with a washer/dryer, so her clothes went directly in. The hot shower she took to remove the stench from her body took away most of the soreness as well. Afterwards all she was left with the horrible goose-egg swelling on her neck, relieved a bit by an icepack, and an anxious sense that she was not alone in San Francisco – that someone was intentionally here to be with her. Nothing could relieve that feeling. It was too primal.

But who? The Scotch hinted at Uncle Bob, but the man from the ferry could only be Uncle Bob if he had found the ultimate 100-pound-weight-loss-in-a-week diet. The shoes, as much as she remembered of them, looked much too narrow and long for Uncle Bob.

Then who?

No, she would not call the Police. Yes, she knew that one should call the Police in such cases because maybe this was part of a pattern and she might hold a piece of the puzzle to be solved. But Lee knew this was not a pattern that involved anyone else in San Francisco besides herself and the man in the shoes. The man who clobbered her ... and maybe the man from the Ferry ... and maybe Uncle Bob. But how could she ever explain to the Police about all of that? As a Police Detective, she knew what she would think of such a story.

She also knew that going to the Police would mean

she would be engaged in their process for hours.

The analgesic she took slowly moved Lee toward what she needed most. While the gradual trip across the country should have removed any time zone issues, she was feeling much too tired for the 11:15pm the clock showed but too keyed up for the restoration of sleep. Her mind raced on and on. Going over and over the evening's events. Faces, senses, smells, intuitions, so much to take from the jigsaw pile and put in place.

Suddenly she knew what she needed to do. Treat herself like she was on a train again. Melatonin, ear plugs, and....

Morning's light gained entry to her room way too early. In her haste to sort out all the details in her mind and her haste to find sleep, she had forgotten to draw the outer drapes. Only the sheers were closed, and while they blurred nighttime activity for anyone outside looking in they were little deterrent to intense inbound light. Perversely, now nearly awakened by the light, Lee drew the outer drapes shut and chose the softer glow of the side lamps. She needed to sort things out, but not in the clear light of day. Sometimes the little things that matter fade before too bright a light of inquiry.

So there in her little, softly-lit cave of a room, Lee sipped some green tea and tried to recall everything about the previous day. The rat, the ferry ride over, the delightful day, the ferry back, the person she thought was watching her, the shadowing of that person, the trip home, the shoes in the doorway, the hit at the back of her skull, the simulation of her as a poor drunk sleeping it off. Somehow it all made sense and somehow it all didn't make sense.

Lee thought her head had cleared with sleep, and certainly the knot at the back of her head was not as painful as it had been. Still the various factors roiled around like they were being stirred in some big kettle of reason. Threat or not threat, followed or not followed, mugged or targeted, known or unknown assailant.

As more than an hour slipped away, she found she was getting no where. She transferred her now-washed clothes to the dryer, fixed a small plate of breakfast, pulled back the drapes and the sheers, and saw it was a blue-sky day outside. Somehow her mood had prepared her for overcast.

But then out of the corner of her eye, down by the corner of the street, she thought she saw someone turning the corner with a walk reminiscent of the person she followed the night before. But there was no way to confirm. He was gone from sight.

Now, if she had been mugged the assailant would have fled the scene. Wait, she couldn't have been mugged. DAMN! She just realized. Nothing was missing. Whoever had done it had taken nothing ... DAMN, DAMN! No, the assailant had stripped her watch from her. She used the watch more as ornament than useful device. Her cell phone was her watch now, but she still wore the watch she had been given on the occasion of her 25th anniversary with the Department. It was engraved on the back, "Det. Lee Comstock, 25 years of Service, N.Y.P.D." So whoever it was took something, but left everything else on her.

If it had been a thief, he would have taken all he could while she was passed out. And he would have probably gone off quickly to fence it all, score, get high, and now be sleeping it off somewhere. But if she had been targeted, not for theft but for some other reason, that person might want theft to appear to be part of the crime. And that person might want to keep an eye on what followed. Did she wake up, did she scream, did she call 9-1-1, did a Police car pull up, did she go into her apartment instead, did she go out again in the direction of the Police station on Valencia, did she draw her blind shut immediately, did she act like a scared victim?

After finishing her breakfast, Lee took another, less-frantic, hot shower. Last night had been to cleanse, this was to soothe and invigorate. She needed to get out, to walk, to get her blood flowing so her mind could be in top form to sort all of this out.

Coming down the stairs to her entry door, she double-checked the outside through the peephole, a practice she had forgotten on her earlier days. No, no one waiting outside, but Yes, a pile of something on the ground. Opening her door inward she saw the pile more clearly, and nestled in the pile, so it could be seen by anyone leaving the apartment but hidden from most passersby, was a squirrel, a dead squirrel, a dead squirrel with a piece of fabric around its neck, a fabric noose around its neck. Reaching behind the door for the broom and dustpan, and up the stairs for the extra recycled Amazon box she had retrieved the day before, she began to clean up her entryway. Unlike the rat the day before which had been stiff, the squirrel was still pliable, not long dead if her detective skills told her anything.

"Detective, can you tell the jury how long the victim had been dead?"

"Yes, by the lack of *rigor mortis* I would estimate the victim had been dead for not more than 6 hours but at least 2 hours."

"Why do you say that?"

"There was some evidence of *rigor mortis*, in the facial region, but no widespread evidence of muscle stiffness."

Using the edge of the dustpan, she loosened the fabric noose from around the poor creature. It was a torn piece of some jeans. She laid it out on top of the other garbage and wanted dearly to examine it. She didn't travel with protective gloves so she would need some instrument to touch the cloth. Then she remembered the ivory chopsticks, several pair, in the drawer in the kitchen. Racing up to the kitchen, she grabbed one pair, and raced back down.

She saw it immediately. The squirrel was gone. She knew it had not suddenly recovered and scampered off. Someone had waited for her to be absent and snatched the squirrel. Looking out from the alcove of her entryway, she scanned the street. A lone, unleashed dog was high-tailing it down the street, a possible suspect until she heard its apparent owner calling from further down the street. As the dog approached the owner, she heard "Who's a good boy?" and not "What have you got in your mouth?"

Otherwise the street seemed empty of anyone who might be carrying a semi-rigorous deceased squirrel.

But the noose of fabric was still there. With the chopsticks (which she mentally noted would be added to the waste pile; she could surely find a replacement pair!) she began to carefully undo the knot and its several loops. The back of the fabric seemed ordinary, but when she turned it over she gasped. There was the manufacturer's label, the familiar logo. "Lee"

In that moment she realized her worst fears were true. Last night had not been a random event. Whoever it was wanted to sent her a message, first with the rat, and then with the attack, and now with the squirrel. I know your name, I know where you live, and....

And she also realized that there was not any way she could go to the Police with this story. The dead rat was bad enough, the left-for-drunk-smelling-of-Scotch was bad enough, but a hung squirrel that had conveniently disappeared, hung with a piece of fabric with her name on it. Psych evaluation time for sure!

The message had been meant for her. And she was not to talk about it with anyone.

She wasn't to talk about being followed, about getting a dead rat, about being knocked out, about getting the dead squirrel, and something else.

But for the life of her, Lee couldn't tell what else. Someone thought she knew or had something that they wanted undisclosed. And they were watching.

She decided that it would be wiser to find somewhere else to stay in San Francisco.

7

IN HIDING

She didn't want it to look like she was leaving. She had checked out the second exit from the apartment, down back stairs and out a back door. Into an alley which made the daily drop of filth on her doorstep look like good hygiene. She had wanted to avoid using that exit except in the most dire of circumstances. This had reached dire.

So, she finished sweeping up the daily doorstep deposit and walked it down to the corner trashcan. She returned to the apartment, drew the sheers, and began to pack her things. Having traveled with a carryon only, she did not have that much. She had counted on the washer and dryer to get her through the longer stay.

BUZZ. The dryer signaled the end of its cycle, and she retrieved the now-sweet-smelling clothes from last evening. She was about to put them on again when she thought better and assembled an outfit from clothes she had not yet worn on her trip. Something no one in San Francisco had seen. And then she filled a simple shopping bag with both some clothes and personal items she would need wherever she went. She left her suitcase right where it was. She left some non-essential items in the bathroom, deciding that she would buy replacement toothpaste and toothbrush so the apartment could still look lived in. She had paid for the whole stay, so why not use it as a decoy.

With the lights still on in the bedroom, she slipped out back, walked a short distance up the alleyway and spotted a restaurant back door with its leaking dumpster and two busboys grabbing a smoke where no clean-air folk would harass them.

"I think I'm lost – can I get out to the street through here?" she said, pointing to the kitchen door.

"No problem by us." One even held the door open for her and as she passed along the inside corridor past the kitchen door and then the restrooms, she could hear a faint wolf-whistle from one of the men to the other. Oddly that felt good for once. She was just another, and apparently attractive, woman to them.

The front of the house portion of the restaurant was semi-busy, but she looked just like a woman returning from the bathroom. She was now very glad she had not packed the suitcase for it would have looked out of place.

As she breezed by the cashier, she looked right at her and said "thanks, everything was great!"

"Come back again."

"I will!"

On the street, now a block away from her own entrance, she headed toward 16th street; she would have to make a choice. Turn right to Mission and take Bart, or turn left to Market, where she would have a choice of streetcar or bus. The bus seemed to make sense because it would be harder for anyone who might somehow be following her to hide on a bus away from her recognition.

Not once did those hairs on her neck alert her to anything wrong. When the bus dropped her off she chose not to take her usual cable car mode but instead walked. She wanted to be close to Union Square but not on it. Lee finally settled into the Grand Hyatt where she registered as Lee Strangler, worried that the stolen watch named her too well. The Hyatt was her choice because it had multiple entrances and exits so no one person could keep surveillance on all of them.

After settling into the room, Lee retraced her route back to the restaurant. The same cashier was on duty, so Lee said, "Breakfast was so good, I think I'll try lunch."

"Sit anywhere you like."

She sat at a table for two at the back, near the hallway to the bathrooms. After ordering, she slipped back down that hallway, out the back door, down the alley, and into her building. She had determined earlier that the second key on the ring from the apartment was that back door. Up she went, turned off the lights, opened the sheers, and then down she went, out the front door (no garbage this time) and off down the street. A quick turn, walk a block, another quick turn, slip into the restaurant, and she was seated at her table before her order arrived.

The waitress said, "Glad to see you are here. I thought maybe you had skipped on me."

"No, just a little problem in the rest room, you know."

"Oh, I know!" the waitress replied, and Lee was not sure if that was sympathy or accusation.

Lee decided to make a day of things off the usual tourist paths. That would take her out of where she might be expected and into areas where anyone other than she who appeared too often would be noticeable.

As a kid her parents had a great poster of the Sutro Baths. Those turn-of-the-last-century baths beneath a steel and glass canopy had been a landmark for decades. A suspicious fire just when their site was to begin development left only ruins. She had read up on the original and the ruins because the whole thing intrigued her as a child and as an adult. She remembered seeing some of the ruins pictured in "Harold and Maude" and had always wanted to see what was left.

So off she went on the Muni light rail out on the N-Judah line to the Pacific, and then a good, brisk walk up to Sutro Heights and the Cliff House. From there, she followed the informal and well-worn tracks to the concrete ruins of the baths. She could still see where the great pool had been, and the smaller pools of varying temperature, and the catch pools that gathered ocean water from crashing waves.

It was a strange place, a place where history and memory connect with reality. It all looked so much smaller, less grand than any of the lithographs or photographs had shown. It was amazing that anything was left, but also so much was gone. The baths themselves, the arcade, the amusement park, the direct trolley line. A location once a focal point was now a footnote.

She wondered if, as she toured the ruins, she would be glad she came. In the end, as she stood above it all and looked out across the Pacific, she had a sense she was very glad she had come to see it. She felt at peace in a way she had not expected.

Down the cliff, back to the MUNI car turn, and back into the city. Her plan was to get some dinner somewhere along the Embarcadero, go back to her place while it was still light, wait to walk up to her door until she could do it with some other people around her so she would not be alone when she got there.

She was also planning on a quick stop at a drug store to get toothpaste, toothbrush, and an automatic timer, all of which would fit easily into her handbag. That errand was actually accomplished at the Safeway just before the Market Street streetcar tunnel. Lee decided she would shop there in its busy anonymity, and then catch a restored streetcar on Market to go down to the Embarcadero. Those were always so much fun.

At the Safeway, she not only bought what she had planned, all of which did fit in her handbag, but she also bought some small food items which she could carry in the small IKEA reusable bag she always had with her. That would give an illusion of getting some more things for breakfasts at the apartment.

Her dinner looking over the Bay was delightful, and she would have liked to have lingered longer, but the lengthening shadows told her she should move on if she were to be home before dark. She caught BART and rode out to her stop, and began to move slowly toward the house. When a group of five people engaged in conversation came along she quickened her pace to match theirs so they right behind her as she walked the block. At her doorway there was enough light to see that no one stood waiting. She let out a sigh of relief, so audible that one of the group turned to ask: "You OK?"

"Now I am, thank you."

She opened the door and went upstairs, checking the little telltales she had left that would alert her to any snooping in her absence. No, the hair across the closet door was still as she had left it. No sign of dusting powder carefully placed on the bathroom floor appeared on the darker carpet. She checked the photo on her phone of how things were in the bedroom. Nothing was changed. Good.

Now to settle in for the evening. She put the timer on the lamp by the bed, and turned the lamp on. Then she manually turned on the lamp via the timer. Perfect. Next she set the timer for Off at 11pm, back on for a quarter hour at 5:30am, and then Off. She moved around the bedroom for several minutes before drawing the heavy drapes, making sure they were not totally closed ... a half inch that did not overlap would be enough so the inside light would be evident to anyone outside.

With everything in its place, Lee left the telltales where they were, moistened the toothbrush, ran the shower for a moment to moisten the walls and curtain, drank some water and left a lipstick stained glass in the sink. She took off one earring and placed it on the bedside table. Then, out to the stairwell, quietly down to the rear, and out the back. Twilight hung in the sky above enough she could see her way easily. She waited by the restaurant door until the kitchen seemed a bit overwhelmed and passed their door and went directly to the table where she had lunch. It was unoccupied. She began to search around it until a waitress she had not seen before came up to her.

"Can I help you?"

"Yes, I was in here earlier today for breakfast, and then later for lunch, and somewhere today I lost an earring. Did anyone find one here."

"Wow, you ate here twice. No, I didn't see anything but I have only been on since 5. Go ask Millie at the Cash Register. She keeps lost and found stuff."

"Thanks."

So Lee explained to Millie, who was not the person on duty earlier, about the lost earring. Millie had no record of one being found, but she said she would leave a note for the day person – did she want the restaurant to call if it was found.

"No," Lee responded, "just tell them to hold on to it if they find it, and I'll check back in tomorrow."

"Will do."

With that Lee strode out of the restaurant with an excuse for one of tomorrow's transits already in place.

She decided she would splurge and hailed a taxi at the next corner. In quick order she was at the Hyatt and tucked into her second home in San Francisco. She suspected the Hyatt did not allow dead rodents to be left by the doors, so she felt much safer.

ACROSS THE BAY

Her sleep was long and wonderful. Her morning shower luxurious as she planned the rest of her day.

She had decided that the Lee sleeping in the Mission should be allowed to sleep in today. If someone were watching her, they could spend the morning in the Mission, while she explored Chinatown. She had some replacement chopsticks to buy.

It was about 1pm when Lee dropped by the restaurant to see if the earring had turned up.

"O, hi again. No, Millie left a note, and we haven't seen it."

"Mind if I take another look?"

"Go ahead."

With that Lee was back by the table, and then quickly down the hallway, out in the alley, in the back door, up the stairs, and drawing the outer drapes open. She made a for-show pot of coffee, and left a partial pot on the drainboard. Then she went out her front door as if she had just gotten going. No, not a shred of debris. She stretched in the sunlight, and set off toward BART.

She was heading over to Berkeley. She had heard so much about Berkeley and its aura of specialness that she wanted to see it for herself.

The trip was an easy one without a transfer. As she stood up by the exit door waiting for them to open as the train decelerated into the Downtown Berkeley station, a voice that seemed to be in her ear said so quietly no one else could have heard:

"Lee Comstock, don't turn around. Walk out of the station and get a juice at the juice bar on the triangle and sit outside."

By the time the train had stopped and the door had opened, she had the sense that no one was standing very close to her at all.

Looking straight ahead, she exited the station, figured out where the voice had named for her to be, and was relieved to see that it put her in a very public place. She was not relieved that someone on BART, in San Francisco, knew her NYPD name. In fact, she was terrified.

She walked into Juice Appeal and up to the counter as if in a trance. When the server asked what she wanted, she realized she had no idea.

"What's the most popular with the cops who come in here?"

"Cops don't come in here."

"Well then, with the students."

"Hey lady, get the energizer," said the person two behind her in line.

"What he said."

A few bucks and 24 ounces later she had a drink in her hand and was heading outside to the few tables set amid the noise and bustle of the traffic from five different directions. She didn't have a moment to relax (if she could have anyway) or check out her surroundings before she heard a voice she recognized behind her say, "Lee, it's OK." It was the full volume of the voice from on BART and it was a voice she knew only too well from back in the Dining Car on that first night.

As CC came around from behind her, he threw something onto the table. It was a leather wallet.

"Open it!"

Inside was the badge and the identification card of

an FBI agent. Charles C. Collingsworth, III.

"See, I didn't lie to you completely. I am called CC. Actually I am called C3 by my family. And when I make them angry I am C3PO, as in 'piss off'"

Lee could not remember a time when she was happier to see someone, and find out who he actually was.

(O, blush! Back on the train that first night, she now remembered, she had a dream about CC. It was R bordering on X-rated. Wow, had she suppressed that!)

"CC, go get yourself a drink and then we can talk. You would look out of place sitting here without a smoothie."

"Ah, cop talk."

"Well, I think you know it."

"I do."

While CC went to get his own smoothie, Lee thought about why she had relaxed so at seeing who it was. Was it because of her own fantasy? Was it because he was FBI? Was it because he wasn't some kind of bad guy? Or was it because all of a sudden she was not in this all alone?

The door to Juice Appeal opened and CC yelled, "What shall I get?"

"Just act dumb and the others waiting impatiently behind you in line will make suggestions."

"OK, act dumb, await further orders."

Ah, former military!

In a few minutes CC emerged with a neon orange something in his hand. He couldn't remember its name. But he said it tasted great.

Lee finally remembered her own smoothie and took a sip. Yes, it was good. Very good.

"Lee, I don't know if you know, but you are in the midst of a heap of trouble," CC began.

Wow, he didn't skirt the issue.

"What did I do?"

"Wait, I didn't say 'you are in a heap of trouble,' I said 'you are in the midst of a heap of trouble',"

"Ah, I need to parse that a bit further."

"Parse? I am dealing with an intelligent person here."

"At least you didn't say 'an intelligent woman'!"

"No, Ma'am"

Ah, former modern military.

In a faked Cuban accent, Lee said, "You got some 'splaining to do."

"OK, Lee, I am an FBI agent. I was assigned, among others, to make sure that a very important scientist, Alexander Nottingham, got to a conference in Chicago...."

At this point Lee suddenly realized why a name on the manifest back out of New York had seemed familiar. Alexander Nottingham, string theory, peace activist. OK. A few pieces were falling into place.

"...but Nottingham has this thing about trains..."

"As do I if you might have noticed."

"I did notice ... and I will get to that in a moment."

Uh, oh, she thought. What does he mean?

"So I had to stay with him while he took the train from Princeton to Chicago without him knowing it. This guy is one bad nerd. He didn't even read his ticket! I was waiting on the northbound platform at Princeton Junction for him to come off the connection from the campus. He had been accompanied without his knowing it by another agent all the way from his apartment. But there he was on the southbound platform, and I am texting the other agent 'WTF?'. Finally he gets over to my side of the tracks and we take off."

"Nice story ... not part of my story."

"Just wait. So, I travel into New York with him. All

is going well, and I hand him off to an agent already waiting in the Club Acela lounge. I need to take care of some other business and not appear to be too connected to his trip. He would never notice, but others might."

"Others?"

"Hang in there. At New York I know he is being handled just fine. Then they start boarding, and he is safely on the train. I get a report about a good looking black woman who appeared suddenly into the mix."

"Hmmm, good looking you say?"

"Don't go all conceit on me! I board as if a complete flake, a latecomer to the party, so I can assess what the situation is. My contact, the Red Cap, hands Nottingham back over to me."

"The Red Cap. Clever. Like I always say, watch out for the person who everyone sees but no one remembers."

"Now I am in close proximity to my charge, and to you. I had wanted the room opposite his, but you had claimed it. How far in advance in did you book it?"

"Look, Mr. Clandestine, you work 30 years for the force and you'll know that 11 months out to the day is when you book it, when it is first on the available list. And want to know why I got Room 2, not Room 1? Because Room 2 is not next to the linen locker, so it is considered a better room!"

"I ... did ... not ... know ... that!" he mimicked.

"So there I am, with my charge locked securely in his room – nerdy as always, shut away from us all. You are in 2, and that guy, Uncle Bob, in 4. I'll get back to him in a minute or two."

"I can hardly wait."

"O, I can tell you, you can!"

"Go on."

"I had already turned Bruce to our cause. There

were a few things in his past he would rather did not come to light. If I were not around, he would be."

"You clever devil, you."

"You were a mystery. I had run the whole manifest prior to the departure and I knew many things about many people. But 'Lee Strangler' existed but had apparently not lived much of a life. I knew she was alive, but not much more. She did not raise flags on any of our watch lists, but she didn't appear on much else either, and that raised a flag in my mind. Did you actually exist?"

"When I first saw you I have to admit I was surprised," he continued, "you were not some empty entry but a very alive, very lively, very appealing human being."

"I appreciate that you did not just say 'appealing woman'."

"For me, people begin as people, and then appealing people begin as appealing people, and if they happen to be women .... well, that's beyond my FBI role."

"Do tell."

"OK, Lee, let me just say that I had a problem that night as I tried to sleep on the train. How does anyone do that, by the way? But just as I would drift off to sleep either the train would jolt or I would start to think about you."

Lee wasn't sure what she should say at this point.

"So, I got very little sleep that night because I was on duty, so to speak. Somewhere around 5 am I finally fell into a brief deep sleep, more of a power nap. I knew Bruce was probably watching out for Nottingham too."

"Why all the fuss over one professor?"

"Because his work in string theory had opened up some major insights into a wide range of applications, from encryption to fusion. He hadn't applied it yet, but the foundation was there, and we wanted to make sure it stayed on our side."

"Did you think he was going to spill some secrets at the conference in Chicago?"

"No, but we were worried someone would want to get hold him and get it out of him. But, no one did, at least not that night, I think. When I woke up on our departure from Toledo, I check on Room 1 and it was still closed, locked, curtained.

"I had Bruce knock on the door of Room 1 while you were off showering. He got the usual grunting response and an order for some breakfast from the diner. And an emphatic order for coffee, black. He got it quickly and delivered it before you got back to your room. Then you went off to breakfast and I left Bruce to keep watch."

"Why would you leave Bruce in charge and go off to breakfast?"

"I'll get to that in a minute or two. But let me first explain why I am here with you. When we got to Chicago, I saw Nottingham leave his room, just before you left. He walked off the train, past Bruce at the bottom of the steps from the car, blended in with the crowd. The next contact picked him up at the end of the platform and shadowed him to the U of C. He went into the building for the conference, checked in at the registration table, excused himself to go to the bathroom, and has not been seen since."

"You mean he has disappeared?"

"Gone, no trace."

"You mean you got him to the conference, and then you lost him?"

"Hey, don't rub it in."

"So, your going to breakfast didn't lose him."

"No, and I had another reason to go to breakfast. I was there to watch Nottingham, but I was also there to watch Uncle Bob."

"Uncle Bob?"

"At least that is what he likes to be called. He is not what he seems to be."

That last sentence struck deep into Lee. There was something about Uncle Bob that had troubled her and this seemed to confirm it. But something more was troubling her now.

"So, how did you find me, and what does this have to do with me?"

"Well, as you might expect, with Nottingham traveling overnight by train, we needed to vet everyone on his part of the train. Oh, if only he would have been willing to fly. But noooo. So, we started with the train's crew and the passenger manifest.

"You probably couldn't tell it, but Bruce was ex special weapons military which means he had top clearance. We got him assigned that night to the car Nottingham was in."

"That explains why I had never seen him before."

"Ah, you just confirmed something for me ... but I will get to that soon.

"So, we went down the manifest, doing a basic background check on everyone in the sleepers, and a deep check on everyone in that particular car. Know what we found?"

"No"

"There were two people with histories that left us wanting to know more. When the paper trails ran out, we were to keep a special eye on them."

"Uncle Bob and who ... was it Hildebrandt or Francis?"

"Again, you keep confirming my suspicions. And no, it was you!"

"Me?"

"You. You and Uncle Bob had appropriate histories for your ages and at first glance would arouse no suspicions. But with the deeper, longer look you two stood out. Robert Farrell and Lee Strangler were just too good to be true. No credit problems. No tickets or citations. No frequent changes of address. No marriages. No divorces. No nothing. The two of you exist, you get mail, you make some little money, you file short form tax returns. People don't live like that."

"Is that a judgment or an analysis?"

"Probably a little of both, and well-proven Bureau statistics.

"So, we decided to watch the two of you because we couldn't get the normal information on you. Were you who you said you were, or were you something, or someone else?

"When Nottingham came up missing, you two became all the more important. We could, and did account for everyone else after the disappearance, but you two again were beyond our immediate reach to talk with."

"What about the others?"

"Everyone else getting off in Chicago had cred with us. For example, the Dutch family came complete with travel documents which had been recorded at JFK as they arrived and background checks in Holland. As peace activists, the parents had been watched by AIVD, and were not connected to anything really worrisome. Hildebrandt got on as scheduled, got off at Toledo for the bus to Ann Arbor, as ticketed. The next morning he delivered his paper to a World Economics Colloquium at University of Michigan as scheduled. And you don't want to know more about the rotund couple in Room 10 ... I just know I will never hear the word 'swingers' and have the same intrigued thoughts again."

"You're kidding me, right?"

"Lee, the FBI doesn't kid!" he tried to say with a straight face.

69

"Go on, but don't gross me out."

"I'll try. So, there were the two of you, you and Uncle Bob. You were this ditzy, first-time traveler, full of antsy energy, or at least that is what you want us all to think. I have to tell you, I bought it right up until dinner."

"That long?"

"Yes, you matched a person with the strange history you had. Someone with little outstanding experience and even less understanding."

"So I did something at dinner that blew that?"

"After dinner, actually. When the coffee began to splash in your cup, you knew a trick about stopping it, something only someone who had ridden trains before would know about."

"How do you know?"

"Because my Dad taught me that one – Dad was a conductor and he showed me that when I was a kid."

"Damn!"

"So, I knew you were not the Lee Strangler you wanted us to believe you were. You knew trains, and therefore you would know more than you were pretending to know. But we knew you had made your connection at Chicago, so for two days we knew where you were. That gave us time to come up with more about you. That was hard going. You had covered your tracks well, which made me even more suspicious. But then we got the break we needed. Any idea what it was?"

"It was my Dad. I mentioned to him about the spoon trick and how I had seen you do that. I mentioned your name, when I said 'Strangler,' he lit up like a Christmas tree. He said 'Can't be more than one family of them in this world. Had a Porter by that name that rode with me many times. Had a whole mess of sons, but only one daughter, and her name was Lee if I

70

remember how he bragged on her and her going to the Police Academy and all.'"

"Done in by my Dad and your Dad."

"Yep, all I had to do was have NYPD run their officers for a female named Lee, and you came up. Lee Comstock, just retired after 30 years. It all fit. And even a brief look at your record told me you were clean."

"Well, thank you, sir."

"Now, all I had to do was to find you at this end of the great American railroad journey. I tried to do a bank trace on credit card use at hotels around here, but that was dead. However, you used an ATM twice in the same neighborhood, so I staked out that ATM and eventually you came by. I followed you and knew where you were residing. Put another agent staked out on you so I could get some sleep myself and check out some other leads.

"You are not an easy person to tail."

"Thank you!"

"You managed to lose him twice, and once you managed to make him. In losing you, he also lost you."

"O, on the boat and up in that park"

"You got it. By the time he got back to your place hoping he would reconnect, you were standing in your doorway, looking under the weather, rubbing your head."

"Boy, how I wish he had gotten there sooner, but finish your story before I tell you mine."

"Then I was surprised to get word from the Bureau that you had used your credit card downtown for a hotel room. What? We had you tucked neatly in bed in your apartment. Didn't make sense. Still doesn't."

"Well, I am soooo good!"

"That may be true, but I'll be the judge of that. OK, your turn."

With that Lee took a deep breath and began her

narrative: Lee Strangler needing a better identity as a cop, long career, retiring as a detective, retirement trip, wanting to be anonymous, hard time getting her mind to retire from duty, sense of being watched and followed, garbage on the doorstep, the rat, the mystery man (now explained) on the Ferry, the attack, Scotch spilled on her, the squirrel, the noose with her name on it, her getting out of the apartment making it look like she was still there, and now sitting with CC, the FBI agent, in downtown Berkeley.

"Wow, you don't live a quiet life do you?"

"Wish I could, or maybe I don't actually wish that."

"You certainly got us on still being in the apartment, but good thinking. I am glad you are safe. I was worried I might lose you somewhere in all of this, and I don't mean just not find you. I didn't want it to be you and I didn't want you to be hurt by whoever it was."

"Thank you! And Uncle Bob?"

"Ah, the old lush ... or was he?"

"Wait a minute, CC, I just remembered something. When I walked by his room when he was up in the Café Club, I was surprised that I did not smell Scotch."

"Ah, the Detective. Stay here a minute," CC requested. With that he was gone down the street. In about three minutes he was back with two glasses in his hands.

"OK, Detective, I've got two glasses here. Tell me, without tasting, which one is Scotch and which one is tea."

"Can't taste them?"

"Not yet!"

Lee looked at the brown liquid in each glass, then bent over to sniff each. A broad smile crossed her face.

"The one on the right is Scotch, and the one on the left is tea."

"OK, taste them."

Lee kept her smile, and went for the one she picked as Scotch first. The smile dissipated with the first sip.

"Wow, wrong!"

She then tasted the other one, and her look became bewilderment.

"You rat. They're both tea!"

"Yes, but you thought one was Scotch. Imagine how the bartender down the street reacted when I said I wanted a Scotch and I was willing to pay for one but I only wanted a couple of drops on my fingers ... and she watched me rub my fingers on a glass, all before she filled up both glasses with cold tea. Hey, I promised I would bring them back in five minutes and I don't want her thinking less of me. I did tip well. Why don't you come along, and we can transition from smoothies to something a little more dangerous"

"But, aren't you on duty?"

"I am, but you're not. You're retired, remember? I can always have some tea."

Lee and CC threw away their smoothie cups and started down the street, each with a glass in hand. They had gotten about three stores along when one of Berkeley's finest stopped them.

"Folks, don't know where you are from, but we don't allow walking around with drinks here."

Lee looked at CC, and shot him a wink.

"Why, Officer, this is just tea. Don't tell me California doesn't allow people to drink tea in public."

"Are you arguing with me, Ma'am? I can smell the Scotch from here."

"Sir, I am not arguing with you. I am just stating the facts, just the facts."

"Don't make me write you citation."

"I think you had better verify the evidence, officer," CC added in.

"Sir, please stand aside and don't interfere."

"No, officer," CC said as he dropped back.

"OK, officer, you are saying I am breaking the law by an open carry of alcohol, is that right?"

"M'am, please don't make this an issue ... pour out the liquid NOW!"

CC interrupted again, "Officer, with your permission, I am going to reach into my coat pocket and produce my FBI Identification. Is that OK with you."

The poor officer now looked perplexed. "OK, but very, very slowly." His hand was on his revolver, its strap unsnapped.

CC moved slowly with one hand, keeping the other hand to his side in plain sight. As he slid the ID wallet out of his coat, he could see the officer relax. He opened the ID and held it for the officer to read.

"Sir, do you mind explain what is going on here."

"Officer, my associate, a retired NY Police Detective, and I are involved in a Federal investigation, and to prove a point I had created these two glasses of beverage. Now if I were to tell you that one is Scotch and one is tea, would you believe that?"

"Yessir. That's exactly what I thought."

"Now, I am going to tell you that you are wrong. If I were to tell you both are tea, would you believe that?"

"No sir. I can smell the Scotch from here."

"Then, sir, with my assurance as a Federal Officer, that both are tea, would you please taste to verify this?"

"If you will be willing to vouch for this to my Sargent."

"No problem."

With that Officer Santiago tentatively tasted what he thought was tea, and looked relieved to find it was. Then he tasted the other, the one he knew was Scotch, and he look shocked.

"Why, that's tea too. What the...."

"Just trying to show Detective Comstock that things are not always as they appear. Now if I were to tell you that one of us is a strangler, would you believe that?"

"Not unless one of you was Special Forces."

"No, not Special Forces, but let me introduce Detective Comstock by her birth name, Lee Strangler."

"Well, I'll be."

"Not everything is as it may seem."

"No sir!"

"Well, I am long overdue returning these to the bar down the street, so I hope all is good,"

"It is, Agent Collingsworth."

"Well done, Officer Santiago, you read my credential and remembered it."

"And you've given me a great story to tell."

"Glad we could help out. Have a good day."

"You too."

Lee and CC headed down the block while Officer Santiago walked toward the triangle, chuckling to himself. In fact, it would be less than 5 minutes later when he would get a chance to tell the story of his encounter with what he called the "tea drunks." Having crossed Shattuck toward campus, an elderly man stopped him and asked about what just happened. He said he had seen that the Policeman seemed to have an encounter with some people drinking on the sidewalk.

"Not the kind of thing I like to see in my town. Have enough of that behavior out of the goddamn students, but fine folks like that. Not in my day."

With that invitation, Officer Santiago told him all about the tea, the Scotch, Agent Collingsworth, Detective Comstock or better Lee Strangler.

"Well, now I have heard everything. Thanks for the laugh for the day, Officer." The old gent, using his cane to steady himself, headed up Center Street, chuckling.

Chuckling until he was out of sight of Officer Santiago. Then he straightened up, folded up the cane and put it into his pocket, and strode off quite purposefully.

But CC and Lee had seen and heard none of this. They had headed to return the glasses to Revival Bar, where a relieved bartender was glad to see them.

"You tipped well, but not good enough to cover the cost of glasses."

"Sorry to worry you. You have been of great service to your country." CC produced his FBI ID, and watched the bartender expression of surprise.

"I won't ask why, or how. But I have a great story to tell now."

"We seem to supplying great stories today," Lee said, "I guess that is our role here."

"You an Agent too?"

"No, I'm just a tourist from New York who has been caught up in a web of international intrigue and violence. That's my story, and I'm sticking by it." Lee knew that sometimes the best bluff is the unvarnished truth because it sounds too unbelievable to be believable.

CC chimed in, "I need to further depose this person of interest. Have you got a place, out of the way, where I can do that?"

"Sure, the Siberian Table, where we seat people who treat us badly. Over there, by the entrance to the kitchen. You'll have the place pretty much to yourselves until about 5:30"

"Good, thank you. And how about two Scotches?"

"On the fingers?"

"No, on the rocks, if that is OK with you Lee?"

"Well, I still have that aroma in my nose, so why not," Lee agreed.

"And make those one Scotch and one tea!" with a wink.

"Two Scotches, [wink, wink] on the rocks, you got it. I will bring them over in a minute. Yes, take that 6 top on the banquette in the corner."

Lee and CC settled in out of the way in the corner, and Loretta (at least that was what her nametag said) brought over the drinks. "For you, Ma'am, Scotch on the rocks, and for you, Agent, something else. Holler if you need anything else."

"Thanks" was their combined chorus.

"Wow," Lee said when Loretta had gone away, "you really are on duty."

"Makes it easier if you are 10 plus years sober and wanting to keep it that way."

"Oh!" Lee knew too, too many police officers for whom alcohol or drugs were an escape from the demands and terrors of the job.

She added, "Well, here's to you, for that and for not being the one who knocked me out."

"I'll drink to that!"

"Let's get back to Uncle Bob. So, he likes to make people think he is a little too into-the-sauce. Makes him seem a harmless old fogey. But then, what is he?"

"We still don't know. He got off the Lake Shore, took the Hiawatha Service train to Milwaukee, picked up his car from long term parking, went to his house in Menomonee Falls, was over at a local VFW post for an evening of cards, checked a mystery novel out of the library ... apparently he loves mysteries about the Florida Keys ... and since then it is like he doesn't exist. No transactions, his car has not moved, no calls on his cell phone nor even a cell tower contact beyond greater Milwaukee. He just isn't, there or anywhere."

"You mean, the FBI is stumped. At least on TV this would be the moment when...."

"What's wrong?"

"It's that feeling again. The hairs on my neck."

77

"OK – I get that sometimes too – so let's keep talking as if nothing is happening, but I will do a slow scan of the area."

Lee started chatting about trivial things in Queens, while CC used the conversation to roll his eyes and look around. There was no one in their section of the restaurant. The big windows gave a great view of the street, and there was no one right along them who triggered anything for CC. But out of the corner of his eye, over by the far corner with Addison, someone had just abruptly turned and was walking quickly away although he had just been waiting with the crowd for the light to change.

"I'll be right back."

CC rushed out of the restaurant and up Shattuck trying to spot the person on the other side. No go.

Returning to Revival, he rejoined Lee and brought her up to date on his rushed exit. He didn't think the person could have seen them from the street – he had looked on his return – and he doubted the man had known CC was following him. No one had looked back as if to determine a tail.

"So, where do we go from here?" Lee asked.

"From here we go back to your hotel, check you out, and get you back to your apartment."

"Will it be safe for me there?"

"Tell me about the apartment."

"Well, you know the doorway. Then it is up a flight of stairs, through an inner doorway, into a small sitting room, which is flanked on one side by a small kitchen and dining area, on the other side by bedroom which faces the street, and between the two areas is the bathroom."

"What's in the sitting room?"

"A pull-out couch. They list the apartment as being able to accommodate four people, but I have no idea how four would actually managed being in it ... it is not that large."

"OK, then here is what I propose. You will go back to your apartment. I will watch you enter from across the street so I know no one is lurking. I will take your back door key and go through the alley and up to your apartment. I will spend the night on the pull-out couch keeping you safe. And all very proper."

"Sounds like a plan. And then?"

"And then tomorrow we are going to follow up on some leads. In the meantime, I am going to see if you remember anything more about your trip and the events here.

"Also, somewhere between checking out of the hotel and getting to your apartment, dinner would be in order. However, while we will dine at the same restaurant, we will be seated at different tables."

"Not too romantic, or is that the playing hard to get strategy?"

"Joke if you want, but I think it best. It will keep us from talking in public, in a crowded restaurant, about what is most on our minds. Speaking of which, things are beginning to fill up in here. We should be going."

CC rose, and Lee followed his lead. They thanked the bartender who gave a wave and "any time!" and walked out onto the street.

"Hey, G-man, watch where you are walking," Lee said.

CC looked down and saw he was standing on a plaque in the sidewalk memorializing an long-ago arrest of Janis Joplin.

"I swear, I had nothing to do with it!"

"Sure, sure."

CC then suggested that rather than immediately descend into the BART station, they should walk to the Rockridge BART station.

"Why?"

"It will give us a chance to seemingly wander through some neighborhoods and get a sense if we are being followed. A stranger will more likely stand out if he or she suddenly is duplicating our random moves."

"Got it. How far?"

"About two and a half miles. You up for it?"

"Actually, some good exercise would be welcomed. Could we maybe go by way of the campus. Seeing that was the reason I came over to Berkeley today."

"Sure, no problem. Actually good idea."

The two of them walked up Addison and onto campus. Lee loved the look of it, with the impressive Campanile towering above it. She also loved the energy and especially when they came upon an area with some tables set up promoting a wide range of causes, plus a small group of protestors worried about some issue. She remembered back to her own days of idealism and disillusion, wondering where that Lee had hidden herself. Part of her wished they had college for adults, where those dormant portions of brain and commitment might be nurtured and flourish again.

It was in the middle of this that CC suddenly stopped Lee, pulled her aside and said, "Don't look."

"You're always saying that."

"No, I mean it. The Dutch family is just coming through the gate and I don't want them to see us together. And I want to know what they are doing here. I thought their itinerary had them out of here by now. Just casually walk up to them, be surprised to see them, and see what you can find out."

"No problem."

"Then just keep walking in the same direction we are going ... head for the bell tower, I will find you."

"Got it."

Lee resumed her walk through the campus activity,

walking right by the Dutch family and then doing a well-presented surprised look, wheeling about, and saying, "Well, Hi there!"

The whole family turned and looked as surprised as Lee had tried to appear. The mother seemed not only surprised, but a little anxious.

"Why, hello. We think we will never see you again. How are you and your trip?"

"Having a great time. Seeing lots of sights. Checking things off my bucket list. Remember that phrase I taught you, 'bucket list?' "

"O, yes, bucket list. We too check things off our bucket list. We went to Napa Valley as planned. Also Sonoma. Very beautiful, much wine to drink. But then forecast for two days of rain. Just our luck, no rain anywhere for months and it rains there when we are there. So we decided to return to the city."

"Beautiful campus, isn't it."

"Yes, the University is very big and very pretty. Much bigger than universities back at home. But we are very happy to see so many … ah, active people … how you say people with opinions?"

"Activists"

"Activists. Yes, many activists working on many things."

"Well, I hope your trip continues to be interesting."

"Dank je. You are the second person from our trip we think we see today."

Lee's ears opened wide at this.

"O, who else did you see," thinking maybe they had spotted CC during his sprint to the bar or elsewhere.

"We think we see Uncle Bob. A man who looked like him was on other side of the street, and we called to him, but he didn't turn to look so we thought it wasn't Uncle Bob. Of course, makes no sense because Uncle Bob was not our train out here. Maybe it is just that all older Americans look the same."

Lee cringed a bit at that last remark, knowing that she had needed to learn to see people as individuals if she was to see them; lumping everyone by how same they looked was not good police work.

"Must be a common look, I guess," and then Lee decided to be creative, "just the other day out here I thought I saw someone else from the train back east, but I was wrong about that too. Thought I had seen CC, you know the younger guy who hung out with Uncle Bob."

"We haven't seen him."

"Neither did I, it turned out. When I got close to the man I thought was CC, I could see it couldn't be he. Wrong eye color, wrong shaped nose. I tried to cover my embarrassment at coming up to him by pretending to ask for directions. Turns out he was from here and was very helpful. Escaped that mistaken identity boo-boo."

"Boo-boo?"

"Faux-pas."

"Ah, faux-pas, that's how we say it in the Netherlands too. Understand."

"As I said, I hope your trip continues to go well."

"Thank you."

"Bye Bye."

"Bye."

While the family huddled to confer as if to decide where to go next, Lee resumed her walk in the same direction she had been headed, using the very visible bell tower as a beacon. The uphill walk was pleasant but she noticed little of it as what the Mies and Pier had said tumbled over and over in her mind.

She was well lost in thought when she heard that familiar voice off to the side of her, "Keep walking straight ahead, and don't look back."

Lee had a hard time suppressing a giggle until CC's voice became insistent, from a further distance, "I mean it! Just keep going. I will explain later."

Now Lee's brain was on active alert mode. No losing herself in thought. But she did not look back. Up the hill until her phone buzzed notifying her of a text message. She took her phone out of her handbag and looked at the message from some unfamiliar phone number.

"CC here. At the next intersection in the paths, take a right."

"OK" she typed in and hit send.

For the next thirty minutes she followed a number of text messages, such as:

"OK - stop. Look around as if not quite sure where you are. Pretending to check directions on your phone. Then take the left"

"Pause and make a phone call ... it could just be to your voicemail, but look like you are talking."

"Up ahead, duck into the convenience store, grab a soda, and come out."

"OK – straight ahead on College"

"Now, into the Safeway on your left. Inside go to the aisle for medicines. Be looking at the pain relievers."

Lee did just as she was told, and as she was pretending to compare generics and name brand products, she heard that familiar voice say "OK, you can turn around."

She was so relieved to see CC standing there, close by.

"What was that all about?"

"You did a great job with the Dutch family, and I want to hear what they had to say because after you walked away and they huddled, they reversed direction and started in the same direction as you were going. I had placed myself along the path ready to greet you when I saw them coming. I had to get myself out of their sight, and I had to make sure you did not react or see them. You were great."

"Thanks. Years of training to follow orders."

"I was hoping they were just randomly following the same route, but I got very worried when you made that fake phone call and they all stopped walking and huddled up again with their map and guide book. When you went in the convenience store, however, they walked right by, and kept on walking. I tailed them for a ways and turns out they headed into house about a block off your route. Down on the corner a woman was sweeping her walk and I asked her if there were any place around there I could rent a room for a couple of days. She pointed to several houses, including the one the Dutch family went into, and said the neighbors all thought those were doing that internet rental thing. She added they were banding together to try to stop it. Students are bad enough, but tourists can be worse. I thanked her and said I think I would rather try a legit hotel. She then told me she liked me."

"She has good taste."

"Or at least she likes people who listen and agree with her. Anyway, I wait a little while longer at a distance, and no one came out so I kept you on your route and paralleled you a block down for some blocks before I got over here. Saw no one making moves to follow you. OK, your turn."

"Not here CC. Let's get somewhere away from people."

"Not a problem. The BART station is just up a short walk, and the platform can be pretty anonymous if we keep our eyes open."

"Maybe I am being overly cautious, or maybe a little paranoid, but I think we should leave the store here separately. We each need to find something to buy, go through separate lines, and then head up to BART on our own. We will find each other on the platform. OK?"

"Not a bad idea. You know, you would make a good cop."

CC was rewarded with a very creative funny-face look.

Lee finally grabbed one of the generic pain relievers and shouted after CC, "thanks for the advice about generics." CC gave an over the shoulder wave as he headed to the next aisle for a couple of protein bars.

As usual, Lee said to herself, I pick the wrong line. CC paid and was out of the store minutes before her. But, that was OK. It would make them look disconnected.

Out of the store, she asked one of the shoppers where the BART station was (she knew full well, but she was into her act) and then walked slowly toward it. At the last cross street before the elevated expressway with BART in its median, as she was crossing she was suddenly aware of a car bearing down on her at high speed, not looking like it would stop. With her heart racing, she jumped up on the curb as the car screeched to a halt on top of where she would have been standing.

A scrawny looking teen boy in the driver's seat rolled down the window and said "Sorry, Lady." It was then that Lee saw the sign under the window: "AAAA Academy of Driving." The apparent instructor in the passenger seat was still in the process of dramatically removing her clenched hands from the dashboard rim and then made a gesture of "sorry."

"Been there myself, no problem," Lee responded. Her heart slowly returned to a normal rate. Looking up and across to the BART platform, she could see CC looking anxiously in her direction. As if to the pedestrians who had stopped to see what the screech of brakes was about, she gave a "thumbs up" making sure CC saw it. He looked relieved.

9

WHO THEN?

Under the Expressway, through the faregate, up the escalator to the platform, Lee was glad to see a San Francisco bound train just closing its doors. This would give her an excuse to linger a while on the platform.

She walked down the platform to where CC was leaning against a support pole, almost to the end of the covered portion of the platform. Lee quietly said, as she passed him by, "let's step outside."

She continued on the platform onto the uncovered portion. Shortly thereafter, CC joined her.

"Why out here?"

"Because outside sound stays more local than in a closed space."

"Ah!"

Lee then began to share her conversation with the Pier and Mies. Their reason for being back in town, their story about thinking they had seen Uncle Bob, her pitching a matching story about mistaking someone for CC.

"Well, done, Detective. You got information, planted some doubt if they ever catch sight of me. But this worries me."

"Me too. But you first. What worries you?"

"That Uncle Bob was possibly seen here. I wouldn't bet on it, but the person I thought I saw across the street from the bar looked a lot like our friend, Bob Farrell."

"That is what worries me too, in part because you

87

are worried. You were suspicious of Uncle Bob even before you met him."

"I need to remind you I was suspicious of you before I even met you."

"Touché. But with me you found a resolution to your suspicions. With Bob, it all remains a mystery. He's not at home, he does not appear to be more or less than a nobody. You and the Dutch people think they saw him here. I just don't like shadowy figures."

"Me neither. But I can't mobilize a Bay Area task force just to look for him."

"No, you can't, but I can bet if he is here, then it has something to do with me. Now there's a horrifying thought!"

"Don't think I haven't just thought of that. You are the nexus of something, and both of us don't know of what."

"Haven't a clue."

"Or maybe you do, but don't know it."

"Always a good assumption in crime work. Somebody knows something that they don't know they know. It only gets bad when others don't know that you don't know what they are assuming you know. No?"

"You lost me somewhere in there."

"What is frightening to me is that others seem to think I have information about something important which I don't even realize I have."

"Oh, yes, that's it. Something, as this all played out, involves you, and you don't know it, but someone else does. I wish that someone else were me, but it's not. That's part of the reason why I wanted a chance to talk with you about the trip, to see if we could together discover what might be forgotten. Now with Uncle Bob coming on the radar, I think it is more important than ever to do that. OK, here comes our train. Walk away from me, say loudly, 'Good talking with you," get on the train and go to the Hotel. I will meet you there."

"Good talking with you," Lee shouted over the squeal of the brakes as the train came to a halt. She went into the second car, while CC went into the first.

The transbay run under the bay was fast and smooth. She saw CC get off at Embarcadero. She got off at Powell, hopped on a just loading cable car and rode up to Union Square. She went to the Hyatt, up to her room, and waited. After about 15 minutes, just as she began to get a little worried, she heard a knock at her door. Looking out the peephole, she saw CC's smiling face. She opened the door with relief.

"OK, here's the deal. I've talked with the Manager. You will technically stay registered in this room for several more days, a temporary hold on your credit card will occur, but then all of a sudden you will be automatically checked out of the room, the charge will disappear, and it will seem like you were not here for that time. Mess up the bed, mess up the bathroom, and grab things you want with you. Before that check out, you will be back to again do a similar daily job of making it look slept in."

"But why?"

"Because we want to confuse whoever it is ... we want them to not think we are on to them."

Lee got it immediately, and followed through. CC directed her to leave alone and head for the neighborhood of the apartment. She was to go to the elevator, take it to the lobby, and check with the front desk to see if she had any messages. She would have one message waiting, one that was purportedly from an old Sorority Sister suggesting dinner the next night; if there were any others, she was to ignore those.

He would follow on the next elevator down, but without stopping at the desk he would be outside before she was. She was to use the motor entrance. He assured her he would be close by. They would separately go and eat in the restaurant she used as her entry to the rear door. CC would leave the restaurant first. Then she was to exit second after a couple of minutes, walk around to the front of her building, let herself into the apartment, close the door, wait at the bottom of the stairs until she heard him coming in the back way. CC would be watching out for her until she went in, return to the restaurant to retrieve something he would leave on his table, duck out the back way and into her building.

Lee slipped CC her back door key before she took one more look at the hotel room to be sure she had taken what she wanted and left what would make it look lived in. She had this strange intrinsic urge to kiss him goodbye, and the very thought of it made her blush. True, with her complexion a blush was less evident, but she felt like she was bright red.

The plan began. She left the room and went to the elevator. As soon as he heard the elevator doors close, CC exited the room checking first through the peephole that no one was visible in the hallway. He took the next elevator down and was well away from the entrance when Lee came out. She looked around to see if she could see him. She couldn't. Her phone buzzed: a text message from CC – "Yes, I see you."

Her looking about attracted the doorman who asked if she needed a cab.

"No thanks, I thought a friend might be picking me up, but I guess I will walk."

"Very good, Ma'am."

She took a leisurely pace, stopping to do a little window shopping as she went down the hill. On the BART platform she spotted CC about a car length away, totally captivated with a newspaper. Her stop was just one station away, so it was no time at all before she was off and heading up the stairs. She continued her relaxed pace, again taking time to look in a few shops until she came to the restaurant. The cashier/hostess from the evening time was back on duty and recognized her. "Did you ever find that earring?"

"No, I didn't. Probably fell off on the street somewhere."

"Just you for dinner?"

"Yes, how about somewhere up front."

"No problem."

Lee figured if someone were following her, someone other than CC, she might as well make it look like she didn't care.

Several minutes later CC entered, spoke quietly with the hostess, pointed to a book he was carrying and then at the back of the restaurant. She nodded, gathered up the menu and the drink menu, and led CC to that back table.

They were in position. Later she would want to know what he ordered. For herself, it was Cioppino, that delightful seafood melange. She indulged in a nice glass of wine from Sonoma, enjoying it with some crusty sourdough bread before the Cioppino arrived. She couldn't see what he was being served, but she was sure the tall glass of dark beverage was not Long Island Ice Tea. CC was absorbed in his book, making notes in it from time to time.

At last he called for his check, settled up, grabbed his newspaper, and hustled out. Lee had wanted a little dessert but he had moved on too quickly. Instead of enjoying a sweet, she got her check, paid, and left with a wave of her hand to the cashier then busy with another customer.

She walked determinedly around the corners onto her block, up to her front doorway, found nothing awaiting her, opened the door, went in shutting it behind her. Then she waited. She had not seen CC.

CC saw her safely inside and then moved from his shadows up the grade to the next street, in half a block, and down the grungy alley. He found the door, used his key, and was in quickly, hugging the shadows all the way. Up the back stairs until he was at the landing with the front stairs.

Lee's eyes had adjusted to the light during this time, so she was able to see CC coming onto the landing. She didn't realize she had been holding her breath, but when she exhaled for so long she became aware of how tense she had been.

CC, adjusting to the dusky stairwells, saw Lee and waved her up. Lee ascended and open the inner door with its key. She entered, turned on the overhead light and was about to welcome CC to her apartment when she stopped in place. She took out her phone, pointed to it and then made the gesture for silence with one finger in front of her lips. They both totally silenced their phones. Then she texted him, "Someone has been in here."

"How can you tell?"

"Tell you later."

CC pulled out his gun, which had been carefully concealed under his arm, and gestured for Lee to stand back. He began to stealthfully explore the apartment. When he was satisfied that no one was in any of the rooms, he texted again, "All clear, but don't talk yet."

Now in his hand was a second phone, or at least something that looked like a phone. He was quietly walking around the apartment looking at this device. Suddenly he pointed at the artificial flower arrangement and smiled, then in the kitchen he pointed at the knife holder and again smiled.

"Bugs" the texts resumed

"What should we do?"

"We could play like we don't know they are there, but that's hard. They don't know I am here, and I want it kept that way. So, you are going to do a little play acting. You are going to get a phone call in a moment. It will be from me. I will say nothing. You will act like there is interference on the line so you can't hear."

"OK"

"So, you will yell into the phone something about not being able to hear, and hang up. Then, you are going to say out loud something about that only happens when ... pause ... and then say something like 'Bugs!' Then get very quiet and take your time until you get to both of them and take them out. I suggest the old toilet flush."

"Gotcha"

Lee waited while she could see CC dialing. Just in time she remembered her silenced phone and switched it back to ring. Her catchy ring tone rang out, and she gave it about half its tune before she answered, "Lee here, is that you, Donna."

"I can't hear you."

Louder "I can't hear you!"

Louder still "I'll have to call you back."

"Damn, Donna, we needed to talk. I got your message at the hotel." CC smiled at this: she had remembered the name on the message waiting at the desk!

"Haven't heard phone interference like that since the mob case, o, wait..." and then she went on silent mode. She did the little motion of twiddling her thumbs. She acted out some charades gestures. Finally she carefully plucked the bug out of the flowers. Then she banged around a bit in the apartment until at last she honed in on the knife rack. With the two bugs in hand she looked to the toilet, shook her head, went to the sink and gently placed them in the disposal, turned on the water, and hit the switch. The final transmission would have been ear-shattering to anyone listening.

"Sure that's all?" Lee asked out loud.

CC closed the door to the bedroom before answering. He also began whispering.

"If Mr. Wizard here is to be trusted. But, just to be sure, you are the only one who will speak in the bedroom, and the bedroom door will be kept closed. It must be as if I am not here. We will talk about bathroom etiquette later."

"Understand," Lee said softly.

"It is possible that your being onto their planted bugs will mean they would need to use some external listening devices or contact devices."

"Exactly who is 'they'?"

"I wish I knew. Whoever 'they' are, they have some good stuff. That wasn't any SpyStore.com equipment. How did you know someone had been in here?"

"Look at that edge of the carpet by the bathroom. See the slight bit of dusting powder? Wasn't there when I left, but a fine film of dusting powder had been on the tile floor of the bathroom. And on this door in the kitchen, see the little hair hanging down here, it was across from the door to the cabinet before."

"I've said it before, but I will say it again, you are good."

"Thank you. Can we talk somewhere without having to whisper?"

"Sure, let's take a shower together."

Lee paused, mulling that over in her mind.

"Can you try that one again?"

"You are going to go into the bedroom, mutter a bit about feeling the city's dirt on you, get out of your clothes, and into a robe. You will also mutter a bit about shower gel, where is that new shower gel I grabbed from the hotel."

"You want me to mention the hotel?"

"They probably already know about the hotel. If not, it will confuse them and maybe have them waste time and resources. If so, what's the deal. OK, mention shower gel, pretend to find it, give a great big sigh, and head off to the bathroom. Remember to shut the bedroom door. I will enter the bathroom with you, so the door will only shut once. Inside you will start to run the shower and we can talk. When we are done, you can take a quick shower."

"While you are doing what?"

"While I am very quietly slipping out to the sitting room. Happy?"

"Yes" although she wasn't sure she was totally happy with it.

OK. CC then did the usual TV countdown in a whispery voice, not speaking two and one at all, and then pointed to Lee.

Lee followed the plan perfectly and before long they both were in the bathroom, Lee perched on the tub rail and CC on the closed toilet seat.

"Lee, what I need you to do is carefully, thoughtfully take me and you back to that train trip. You were the person closest to Room 1. What do you remember?"

Lee recounted it all. Her trained eye, even in retirement, was a great asset. She went over it from start to finish. But nothing stood out. Still, she had this nagging feeling she was not remembering something she saw.

"OK, let's do it again."

Lee knew this technique. She had used it many times. Have a story told over and over again not just to see if the details remained the same but not with a rehearsed sameness but to also see if new things could be remembered once the old things had become routine in their re-telling.

The shower was getting a little long even by Lee's

standards for self-pampering nights. She suggested to Lee that more than telling it one more time, she needed to sleep on it all now it had been brought to the surface. CC agreed and slipped out of the bathroom, lowering the volume of water just before he opened the door, gesturing to Lee to turn it back up as he closed it behind him. The shower sound would remain constant.

Very shortly thereafter a thoroughly wet, but not relaxed, Lee came out robed and toweled. She waved to CC, and mouthed "nite nite," and he mouthed "sweet dreams." She gestured about turning out the bathroom light and fan; he mimed yes for the fan and no for the light. He didn't need to be banging around in the dark overnight in that bathroom. As soon as she had gone into the bedroom and closed the door, he visually double-checked the hallway door and then arranged himself on the couch, not daring to pull it out for fear of the strange sounds it might make. He turned out the lights in the sitting room and saw the narrow slit of light under the bedroom door. When it went out, CC relaxed toward sleep, glad he was not known to snore. When he heard the rasping sounds coming from the bedroom a short time later, he realized he needn't have worried.

Sleep came soon for both of them. They were tired from the whole day. End of day, even with the quick shower, had re-awakened some of Lee's ache and stiffness from before. She lapsed toward dreams; he drift toward an aware sleep. He had been trained in how to be alert even when asleep.

10

UNCLE BOB

CC was aware before he was awake. By the time his eyes were open all of his senses were on overdrive. He sensed it before he even heard it. And he was bolt upright by then.

Someone was doing something at the back door. The muffled sound was echoing up the stairs and through the door right by where CC's head had been. It was a sound that would never have been heard way in the bedroom. It was barely discernible here. But it was there nonetheless. Not a brute sound of pry bar. Certainly not the splintering sound of wood. Rather the slight metallic scraping, popping of lock picking.

CC put his gun back in his arm holster, pulled on his coat, and slipped on his shoes. His deft footwork about the apartment earlier had also shown how light and quiet he could be in these shoes. They looked like standard oxfords, but they had special rubber soles. He was a real gumshoe with these.

In coming up the stairs earlier he had noticed that one stair had a bad creak to it, while two others moaned a bit on the handrail side. He slowly undid the lock on the hallway door, and then waited a long moment, so there would not be any profusion of sound. The slight noise below did not pause. He crept the door open just enough to let him pass, and he lowered himself down the stairs being careful to avoid those noisy treads.

He was on the last step before the lower entryway landing when he heard the lock snap, the dead bolt pulled back. One hand went for his gun, the other for his phone. Both were in position as he watched the doorknob slowly, silently turn, its flimsy latch retreating into the door.

Its security now breached, the door itself began to slowly open outward. Whoever was opening it was in no hurry, more worried about sound than about speed. The exterior entryway, extending on both sides about the same depth as the door's width, kept the widening gap a chasm of darkness. Whoever was opening the door was standing so the door blocked any view because that gap showed no person. No one was peeking around to look inside. But slowly the edge of a person's waist began to show, a bit rotund. By keeping to the hinged side of the door, CC could see the outline of the person slowly being revealed without being seen himself.

Now was a time of calculation. Sensing when the right eye of the person outside could first see into the portion of stairway where CC was positioned. Sensing when CC, by a quick move, could suddenly face most of the intruder. Sensing when his left hand, with its phone programmed and primed to become a strobe light could jab into the opening, into the face of the intruder, and deliver its blinding flash. Sensing when his foot could kick the door fully open, probably hitting the night-thief squarely. Sensing when his right hand with its readied gun could draw down on the blinded, startled, door-slammed person.

The door stopped in its opening motion for just a moment. CC tensed. Was the person on the other side doing similar calculations? Would something be thrown into the gap to test its emptiness? Would a weapon appear ready to strike anything behind the door?

Then the opening motion began again and CC focused on what he was seeing: a bit of waistline, a tensed elbow, a bit more arm, the first hint of shoulder and wrist. At the barest suggestion of an ear, CC acted. FLASH! CRASH! "Stay where you are and drop any weapons."

"No, sir, stay where you are, and drop your gun."

The lingering effects of the strobe, which blinds its victim at the cost of slightly stunning its user, echoed in CC's eyes. His kick to the door had been less successful than planned because it would appear the person on the other side reacted instantaneously to the flash and stepped back, so the door had crashed into the entryway wall, embedding its knob into decaying brick, while CC suddenly off balance from the kick was up against the stairway wall rather than in a full stance.

Had this been a high school wrestling match, at this point the referee would have blown the whistle, indicated there was no score or advantage, and put the two wrestlers back to the sides to come out again. But this was no high school wrestling match.

Two men, each with a powerful gun pointing at the other, one off balance, the other nearly blinded, each claiming the upper hand.

CC decided to go the full bluff route. "FBI, throw down your weapon, and put your hands on your head."

"Shit!" was the response.

Now, CC expected to hear something quite different, everything from a gun shot, to a defiant "Yeah, right!" to "Up yours, Fed."

He did not expect to hear "Shit!"

And then his nostrils finally got his brain's attention. Useless in the rest of the encounter because he was not sniffing out a criminal, CC's nose went along for the ride until now.

"Not shit," CC's mind was saying, "Scotch!"

"Bob. Robert Farrell, you are under arrest for assault on a federal officer."

"Charles Collingsworth the Third, you are under arrest for impersonating a federal officer."

"What the..."

"Who's the impersonator, eh, Bob? Uncle Bob?"

"Hey, Droid, I'm CIA. Want to see the creds?"

"How about this, I show you mine if you show me yours."

"So we can play doctor? What a dance-partner kind of Federal Bureau of Insanity thing to say."

"At least I'm not a Crybaby in America kind of guy."

"Fucking Buttheads of Incest"

"Caught in Amnesia"

"Fathering Bastards of Interest"

"Capturing in Astonishment"

"OK, don't need to see the credentials you know enough pass-slurs to qualify."

"Not doing so bad yourself. Want to come up."

"Sure, why not, I could use a little nip of Scotch."

With CC leading the way, the two started up the stairs.

"Hey, be sure to close and lock that door behind you. We don't want any KGB to crash our party."

"If only you knew."

Once in the sitting room with the lights on, CC gestured for silence to Bob. He knocked lightly on the bedroom door, and then opening it slightly he cooed, "O, honey, we have company."

Lee was not amused. Having slept through the whole melee at the bottom of the stairs, she was not happy with the light streaming in. The clock said 4:04. "Just a minute." She struggled to the surface of awareness, pulled on her robe, and rubbing her eyes she opened the door completely and gazed into the brilliance of her sitting room.

"Lee Strangler, aka Lee Comstock," CC said, with a slight bow, "may I present Uncle Bob, aka the CIA."

"O, shit" Lee responded.

"That word keeps coming up tonight. I suspect it is a word we will often use to describe the events of the evening," CC added.

"Uncle Bob, so glad you could drop in."

"Actually it is more like he broke in."

"Uncle Bob, you got some 'splainin to do."

"My dear Lee, so good to see you again. Yes, as this Figurative Blob of Injustice agent just said..."

"I thought that was all behind us."

"We shall see, but as I was saying before being so rudely interrupted, I am Robert Fredericks, better known to my associates as Uncle Bob Farrell, agent for the Central Intelligence Agency, into whose trusted care one Alexander Nottingham was placed so he might safely get to a conference in Chicago and not be spirited away by the forces of evil."

"Into your care? I think not, " CC objected.

"Fraid so, compatriot. But it would appear that those in the know not only did not trust the FBI, they did not trust my beloved CIA either. They assigned both our agencies to the same tasks, and in divine retribution, we both failed."

"I am not so sure I would call it failure," CC responded.

"It is true that we don't know where Nottingham is, and we don't know who took him or why, but we do know that no one claims to have him, and in fact I happen to know that several governments of Asia and the Middle East are all working hard to try to figure out what we did with him because he disappeared on them too just as they had plans to entice or encourage him to be helpful to them," Uncle Bob continued.

"So, we failed and we succeeded, all at the same time. Well done! Think what we might have been able to do if we had been communicating with each other," was CC's commentary.

Lee decided she had enough of this chatter. "Boys,

not another word out of either of you until you are spoken to. I'm putting on some coffee, and if I hear so much as a word out of either of you, no coffee for you. And Bob, I'll rub some Scotch on your collar if you like."

"O, no, my dear, behind the ears, *behind* the ears."

"Shhhhhh"

Lee went off to make the coffee, and when it was brewing, she stood in front of the two agents and proclaimed, "I am off to the bathroom, and no, I do not need any supervision or help. If you want to help, while I am in there you can snoop all you want and figure out something to have with the coffee so the acid wash I am making won't totally destroy our little tummies. And one more thing, I don't want to hear anymore FBI, or CIA. Want to use acronyms, all you need to use is USA. At the NYPD we had too many bad results from parts of the whole thinking they were more important or better than the rest. In this apartment, it's USA or nothing. Got it?"

The two men nodded in agreement. By the time Lee was back, dressed and looking much fresher, a nice plate of cheese and sausage and cut up fruit had appeared. The coffee was dark, strong, and very good.

They all three actually talked about the food and coffee for a few minutes before getting back to the issues at hand.

Uncle Bob started it off, "So, what tipped you that I had been in here earlier."

"The hair on the cupboard door was undone and the dusting powder from the bathroom floor was on the rug edge."

"Hmmm, I did open the cabinet, but I never went in the bathroom. And how did you find my bug?"

"Don't you mean, bugs?"

"No, I only planted the one in the flowers – bug, planted, flowers – get it?"

"Bob, too early!"

CC chimed in, looking much more chipper than a few minutes earlier, "so I guess we have to assume that either the CI ... I mean a branch of the USA security team ... is not telling us the truth"

Lee shot him daggers.

"Let me begin again. Based on what has been shared here, it sounds like it is safe to assume that more than one person was in this apartment before Lee and I got here tonight."

"Much better!" Lee affirmed.

"So, who was that? Any idea, Bob?"

"Not a clue. For a long time, we had both of you on our radar. Then we found out you were FBI, CC, and that cleared you, or sort of."

"Careful, Bob."

"What I mean by that is the appearance of an FBI agent on a manifest of a major security person of interest raised our antenna. Since we had not been told about you, we couldn't be sure if you were there to help or hinder our work. You might have been there to do the same we were doing, getting Nottingham to his meeting. Or, you might have been there to help him get away for some reason. Or maybe you were there for some witness protection deal, which meant we had competing interests on the same train. And that could mean divergent vectors of threat and control.

"Now, Lee, you were a cipher for us. You didn't look bad in any way, but you didn't look good in any way. That first night I detected you were playacting a bit. I saw you sniffing your way down the corridor, not something a nobody would do. You worried me. And then at dinner,"

"I know what is coming. The spoon trick."

"Yes, the spoon trick. I didn't know of it before you did it, but I knew it was a very informed action, not something one would just discover on their own. I put out some feelers and found it was a railroad and steamship trick. I then followed up with some calls to contacts in the railroad and shipping veterans groups. Those guys love to talk and have too much time on their hands so they will give you all you want. Turns out we found someone who said we were the second people interested in this in a week. That piqued our interest too."

"Let me clear that up now, Bob," CC broke in, "that person was probably my Dad."

"Yes, it was. So your name came to us from two directions. If you weren't FBI, you would have gone to the top of our list. As it was, it was verification that we were on to something. So, all we had to do was ask your Dad 'what did you tell the other person.' He told us about Lee's Dad, and we had the whole picture, or did we?

"What is a great NYPD detective doing in the midst of all of this? They claim she is retired, but she is not wearing her retirement like a badge. She is hiding it, and she is hiding all of her background. What's that about?

"Of course, none of this would have mattered had Nottingham gotten to the conference. He would have shared the portion of his research that we wanted him to share as if it were the sum total of what he had discovered; we had hopes that the interested parties would have gone away, thinking there was nothing of interest to them."

"So," queried Lee, "the conference was all a set-up, a charade of sorts, with lots of other speakers but in fact Nottingham the *raison d'etre* for it happening. Without him there, what did you have?"

"You had a pretty empty program, filled out by a number of Doctoral candidates who thought they were doing great things in String Theory, but if Nottingham had shown up his throwaway material would have blown them all away. He would have shone, but only to the extent we wanted him to shine. Let's just say, it was a disappointing afternoon, with a number of foreign powers not satisfied, still thinking they could exploit or even turn Nottingham."

"So, where is Nottingham."

"We haven't got the vaguest notion."

"So what are your theories?"

"That he needed to disappear for some reason, and his escape from the conference made that possible. Or that someone snatched him. But what perplexes us is that we have no credible information about any of those foreign powers having operatives within miles of the conference. None of it adds up."

CC had held his tongue for a long time, letting Uncle Bob be the authority of the moment. Now he could keep quiet no longer. "There are a few pieces of this puzzle you need to see, or at least hear, and the puzzle master, or puzzle mistress, is right here in this room. And it isn't me, and it isn't you Bob. The professionals have failed, but the retired cop may have some answers."

"Why do you say that, CC?" asked Bob.

"Think about it … I am here because of Lee. You are here because of Lee. Someone else broke in here, and someone else planted a bug here because of Lee. And there's more. Let Lee tell you."

"OK, Miss Strangler, tell me."

"First of all, Uncle Bob, I need to know. Did you have anything to do with me being clobbered over the head the other night?"

"I swear, we had nothing to do with anything like that. This is the first I have heard of it. Here comes an embarrassing confession, and if it leaves this room I will deny it was ever said. We, and by that I mean the CIA, have been one step behind these FBI guys all along the way. Just as I was second to discover who you really were, by the time we got here we started getting reports that you were being watched. It took us a day to determine you were being watched by the likes of CC and his friends. This has not been our finest hour, or day, or week, or even month."

"Second, were you in Berkeley yesterday?"

"Got me on that one. Yes. I had someone tail you to Berkeley, and I went over to make sure you were the same, sweet, little Lee I had met on the train. Yes, you looked the same, but you were hanging around with this guy. Then I found out you two were onto my Scotch act and knew I had been made. CC, you almost caught me on the street, and later I had to get out of sight of those Dutch tourists. It was a bad day, and then I see you come home and I start listening in, and the next thing I know it feel like I am having my eardrums ripped out. No, not my best day, not my best night. Lee, maybe you got it right, retire!"

"OK," Lee began, "Our story so far. The Lone Ranger and Tonto had arrived in the frontier town of San Francisco."

"Get serious."

"I am being serious. This is a long, drawn out tale, much longer than the few days in which it happened. There are cliff-hangers and more, " Lee narrated. She got herself into a comfortable position in the lounge chair and settled in for the long-haul. From the years in police work, she knew if she were awakened in the middle of the night and pumped with coffee, she would be running at full speed for hours, even a full day if needed, before she would crash.

Once comfortable, with her coffee cup in her hand, she began to tell the story one more time. CC was quick to note in his mind that it was essentially the same story he had heard thoroughly twice through. She told it slightly differently, but the basic facts remained the same. He thought she would be a formidable witness under any cross examination. Unshakeable.

It took nearly an hour for it all to come out, and often Bob just grunted or shook his head. He made passing comments about the rat and the squirrel, making sure she knew he had nothing to do with either of those. When she was done, Bob looked her squarely in the eye and said, "I am now more worried than I was before. There is something very amateurish all of this, and that always frightens me. Professional criminals, even diabolical diplomats, have a method to their madness. This falls outside of that."

"What makes you say that?" Lee asked.

"Dead rodents, knocking you out but only taking your watch, trying to pin it on me with the Scotch ruse. Here is what I figure. Whoever it is wanted to scare you but in a way that you would not go to the Police. Had to think anyone would hesitate to tell the cops about a rat and a squirrel. If it had been a moose and a squirrel, we would have had a Hollywood type on our hands."

"Bob, get serious."

"Couldn't help myself. The watch was the one thing on you that had a name other than Lee Strangler on it. Whoever knocked you out had not yet figured you for a cop. He, or she, needed that other name and poof, you're made. I'll bet there was a call back to your old precinct from some alleged superior officer, probably claiming to be IAD, wanting to know about you. And some friendly desk Sargent told all about where you were."

"I'll check that out, I can tell you."

"I am also guessing that whoever it was asked if there were a way to get in touch with you, and they were given your cell number."

"Yeah, that explains a call on my Queens cell phone from a San Francisco number that I didn't answer but didn't leave any voicemail."

"Yes, and with some simple software checks, that caller would know the cell tower here where it pinged. That would verify it was you, you from Queens, here in San Francisco, you here in this neighborhood. Just had to hang out in the neighborhood and keep their eyes open until they spotted you. And it had to be someone who would know what you look like. Have you still got that number? It was probably a cheap burner job, but we need to check it out."

"Sure, it's on my phone. I will get it for you."

"So, we are looking for someone who knew you as Lee Strangler, knew you were headed to San Francisco, and knows what you look like. Now, let's start to create a list of who that might be."

CC jumped in, "We can divide up the list and do some background on everyone on the list. Maybe the phone will help us out too, even if it is a burner."

"Team work time," Lee added. "But, one thing you didn't mention was the big question for me: 'why?'"

Why IS the big question. It's a question of motive – do you know something that would make a difference to someone? Wish we had some idea of what that might be. By the way, I should tell you that we did check out where you were while Nottingham was headed for Hyde Park. You may have thought you were anonymous in a city far from home, but when we showed your ID photo around, you were seen sitting by the Lake at the time Nottingham disappeared from the conference. So we know you are clean. The motive is not your involvement in the disappearance, but something else."

"Well, it sure is good to know I am not a suspect."

"You were until we put the pieces together. We had to know it was not that some of those involved were trying to silence another involved. Nothing pointed to you," Bob assured Lee.

"So, if it is not a matter of insider information, it must be a matter of outsider information," Lee responded, "and I am the outsider ... but as an ex-cop I am another kind of insider. If someone involved thinks I know something, then because I was a Detective I become doubly dangerous."

"You are wrong, Lee," CC quipped, "you may have officially retired but you will never be a Detective in the past tense. And you have shown that, and you know that. From the moment you got on that train, the tourist Lee Strangler and the retired Detective Comstock fought for your mental attention. You may leave the job, but the job never leaves you."

"I am learning that the hard way, and this time something about the part that refused to retire has gotten me into the middle of a great mystery."

"So, let's solve it together."

"More coffee?"

"Yes, and something more to eat too, if you have anything."

"I do, and I'll set it out in a moment. But first, I wish we would make that list, and then after we have eaten a bit, I have another request."

Lee, CC, and Bob started the list, focusing on some names Lee knew, and on some she did not know. The others were people at the Conference from which Nottingham had disappeared. The abductors would surely have been there. But someone who knew what Lee looked like would have to mean that someone on the train was also connected to the plot. They knew from earlier investigation that no one from the train was at the Conference at the time Nottingham disappeared. So, they were looking for more than one person. And those several persons would be revealed if they could detect the connections.

So, a second list was developed, not of people but of connective themes, such as common nationalities, shared friends, interlaced finances, cooperating scientific research.

The two lists were compared. Some of those on the train were crossed off because of either or both of two factors: government clearance, no link to any of the connective scenarios.

CC volunteered to try to follow the names left in the direction of any of the collective themes.

Bob agreed to take the other direction, developing the themes to see if any of the names appeared in the process.

By that time, Lee had brought out any and all of the foods that might have any appeal at that hour. She also chimed in as the two assignment groups were developed with insight and reservations. But she finally had one question of them both, "Where do I fit in?"

"You, my dear," Bob said in his best Uncle Bob voice, "you are going to continue to be bait, lure, allure, interest."

"You mean 'target' don't you? Want to paint a bullseye on my back?"

"No, no. CC and I will make sure that you are never out of sight of one of our agents. But we two are going to have to disappear. If someone knows what you look like, that person might also know what we look like. Even if they think of us as old-geezer Uncle Bob, and CC the exhibit designer, they would find it odd if they were to see us together with you. We shall disappear by way of the rear entrance just before dawn. But before we do that, I have something for you to do."

"Yes, what is that?"

"Go down your front stairs, don't turn on any light down there, open the door slightly and look at the latch and the strike. And the cylinder. Shut the door, lock it, and come back and tell me what you see."

Lee did as he said. She was back quickly and quietly. "Slight scratches on the strike, front of the latch hole, horizontal. Slight scratches on the latch, vertical at the exposed point when the bolt is thrown. And here, take a look at my finger."

Bob and CC looked at the offered finger. "Yes, graphite. Someone tested the bolt to see if it could be moved. Then the cylinder was prepped and picked. That is how our second visitor entered to plant the bug. It was that person who went into your bathroom and left the dusting powder on the rug. I suggest you not use your toothpaste or any other item in the bathroom that would go into you or your mouth."

"O dear. Now I am glad that CC made me feel rushed over the quick shower I took, and I didn't want to make it longer by flossing and brushing. Instead I just grabbed a mint from my purse and figured I would catch up in the morning."

"And I know that whoever it was did not try the back door. When I came into through the back door the first time, there were no such signs on the locks back there. When I tried to come in the second time I saw that some little dust I had left had not been disturbed. Front door, one attempt. That doesn't mean we won't keep an eye on the back too, but so far the front door is the entry of choice, as well as the entry of threat and warning."

"Order of business for the morning – new toothbrush, new toothpaste!"

"Please let us test the old ones."

"OK - and let me know what you find."

"Didn't you have a request of us, Lee? You

mentioned it earlier."

"I do have a request, but not now. I thought my hyper energy would keep me going for the whole day and what I want will require energy. But I am crashing. I need some sleep."

"OK, we will let ourselves out the back. I have already put people on the back," was Bob's comment.

"And I have some people on the front," CC echoed. "We even let them know about each other so we won't have another event like what happened to the two of us. Now we, and our people, have things to do. Two lists, two directions. Onward!"

"Good night, Lee. Know that by the time you awaken, refreshed, we might have some new information. But we will not be coming here again. You will instead go down to your hotel, make the room look used, and check at the desk for messages. Your friend, a ... Janice, from the old neighborhood, will leave you a message about where to meet us."

While Bob prepared to leave, CC looked less interested in leaving. "You know, until someone tried to break in on us, I was enjoying my sleep on the couch with you in the next room."

Bob put an end to all of that with "Come along CC, walk Uncle Bob home. I think he is about to become unsteady on his feet from too much Scotch." With that Bob took out a small vial, let two drops fall to his finger, and dabbed behind his ears.

"Good night, Lee," was all CC could get out before a tipsy Uncle Bob dragged him toward the back stairs.

"Night you two! Night, CC!"

11

After she heard the two of them descend the back stairs and the door latch after them, Lee tidied up briefly, and then went into the bathroom. She reached for her toothbrush and toothpaste to remove the much-too-long-neglected mouth taste she had, with overtones of coffee and cheese. Then she remembered she had given them to CC. Her mouth felt terrible. She thought about what she could use instead.

It came to her in a flash. In the refrigerator, there before she arrived, was one of those freshening boxes of baking soda, the kind with the mesh panel to allow 'frig air to interact with the soda to take odors away." She grabbed it out of the 'frig and opening the top took a tablespoon's worth from the far side of the box. Back in the bathroom, she used a wet finger to grab up some of the soda to form a paste, which she applied to her teeth with some vigorous movements of her hand. Her mouth must have been somewhat acidic because the soda began to foam a bit. She rubbed, it foamed, until she had the look of a rabid dog. Looking at herself in the mirror, she began to laugh, the first laugh she had enjoyed in too long. She had not realized how all of this intrigue and threat had drained her. But the way her laugh became almost hysterical told her all she needed to know. She felt as mad as her foaming mouth made her look.

Sleep, that was the answer. Sleep, knowing that CC and Bob were working away on it all. Sleep, long, deep. But was she safe? They had promised she would be watched. But was she really safe?

She put out the lights in the bathroom, and then the sitting room, after assuring herself that the inside door was securely closed, locked, and chained. Then in the bedroom, she straightened the bed linen she had abandoned when CC had awakened her to re-introduce to her to Bob. She turned out the lights but did not go directly to bed. She slowly opened the heavy drapes about six inches, and then parted the sheers just enough to get a view of the street below. Nothing to see. No one there. Something moved! O, a tuxedo cat on the prowl, with a rather nice looking collar. Someone's pet. Nothing else, no one else, which worried her. She thought she would see someone watching her place. She had hoped she would see someone watching her place.

She sadly and slowly pulled the heavy drapes shut, and then let the sheers fall back shut, and slid herself into bed. There was a heavy knot in her gut because she felt that CC had let her down and that she was not as safe as she would like.

BUZZ - a text message arrived, its notification turning the ceiling a ghostly shade of green. She swiped across the screen to unlock the phone and tapped to get to her messages. The little number "1" was positioned right by CC's name and phone number. Another tap and the message popped up, right below the earlier exchanges she and CC had used for silent communications. It read "my contact out front says to tell you that you opened the drapes and then the sheers and saw the cat go by. I hope that lets you feel well cared for."

"I love you for that!" she keyed in and sent before she thought about it. The sentiment arose from her feelings more than her brain. She blushed a bit seeing it pop up with the time of transmission.

Now sleep came easily. Deep, deep sleep. Deep, safe sleep.

It was close to noon when Lee awoke. She remembered she had dreamed a strange dream more than once. Each time she was watching herself brush her teeth. The first time with her finger and soda that created foam. Then a second time with her finger and toothpaste. Then a third time with a toothbrush and soda and the foam. A fourth time with a toothbrush and toothpaste but still the foam.

"I never knew I cared that much about oral hygiene," Lee thought to herself. But then she remembered another part of the dream: after she brushed her teeth, she was walking toward someone starting to plant a kiss. Once a kiss on the cheek of her father. Next a kiss on the neck of a boy she had dated in high school. Then a prim kiss on the lips of a college beau. And the final time, the last time, it was a full on, open-mouth kiss on CC.

"Oh, my," escaped her lips as she remembered.

The dreams both excited and frightened her. Why such a mixed reaction? She didn't know.

But she did know that it was time to get ready for the day ... there was toothpaste and a toothbrush at the hotel, and a note from CC should be awaiting her there. She would take a few things in her purse and get cleaned up there. Too many little details to keep worrying about dreams. Once dressed and with her handbag stuffed with what she wanted, she flung open the drapes. The BUZZZZZ of the phone came less than 30 seconds later. "Good morning! Hope you slept well. Lots to tell you. See you soon."

A smile spread her lips revealing her poorly cleaned teeth, but she felt very alive, and awake.

Making sure that the apartment was in order, she restored her telltales, and then went out. At least today there was no garbage in the entryway.

It was a brilliant noontime and she squinted a

moment going into the sun. She pulled her sunglasses out of her handbag and they stopped the squint. They had been a treat for herself, a designer pair, and she felt very fashionable in them.

She decided to walk up to Market Street, her legs needed the exercise and her lungs needed the air. There she caught an F line car downtown to Powell, got on a cable car to Union Square, and then walked over to the Hyatt. She went up to her room and found it already had been freshened by the maid. It would be quick work for her to make it look like she had slept there, ready for the next morning's freshening. But, her teeth were a greater priority. That mission accomplished, she bathed, brushed, powdered, and all, before slipping into a new outfit. Then she mussed the bed and scattered some other things about; lipsticky lip prints on a glass, some tidbits of random notes on scraps in the wastebasket. She and the room were ready for the day. She went down to the lobby and asked at the desk for messages.

There were two.

One from "Janice" was about how wonderful to find she was in town and could they meet for lunch. A place and a time as mentioned.

The other one was unsigned and simply said "Hope you slept well wherever you slept."

It sent chills down her spine. She folded it carefully and put it in her bag. She asked the clerk if she remembered who had left it. Oh, sometime this morning just after coming on duty at 7am she had found it on the counter with Lee's name and room number on it. That's all she remembered.

"Thank you. If you remember anything else, would you leave me a message, please."

"Of course, Ms. Strangler."

Lee had about an hour before the mentioned time

to meet "Janice." The location was a vegan café. Lee felt more like having bacon, or smoked salmon, than some multiple of beans, but she realized that anyone who had researched her life would never expect her in a vegan place. Good choice, CC.

She used the time to do some browsing in a couple of artsy shops, but she found it hard to concentrate. Too much floating around in her head.

It was in the second shop that it happened again. She felt that tingling at the back of her neck, right above the now grey-bluing lump; those hairs had her attention. They also had the attention of her gut, which was again in a tight-knotted panic. She had to get out of there, almost feeling claustrophobic.

She stood under the store's arcade, breathing deeply and settling herself. Old yoga mental exercises came automatically to life, and she began to relax. In about 5 minutes she felt close to all-better, but she felt drained as well. Hungry? Emotion reserves depleted? Still tired? She didn't know.

But now she would need to hurry along for lunch with "Janice." She stepped out onto the street, squinted, reached in her bag, "DAMN!" She didn't just think it, she said it, loud enough for others on the sidewalk to turn and look.

She must have left them in the shop. She would have to go back in there. She didn't know if she could do it. But those glasses. She just had to.

So Lee forced herself back into the shop, striding along looking straight ahead, all business, to where she had been browsing. No glasses.

She asked the nearby clerk, but he had not seen any glasses. He asked the other clerk who similarly had not seen the glasses. "Sorry."

She tried to remember. Yes, she had taken them off when she had entered. She had been wearing them in the street but taken them off when she entered. But that is the last she remembered having them.

$300 down the drain, and now she was left squinting in the sun, looking for the shadiest route. Her squint made her face tighten up, making her look cross. She noticed people stepped away as she walked along and when she saw her face reflected in a window she knew why. Hers was a face of pain, fear, fatigue and something like despair. She would have avoided herself if she could. Using that same mirroring window, she adjusted her face: she relaxed, took several deep breaths, and told herself that she could be late for lunch. It would all be OK.

It had been OK for thirty years of police work. Through long foot patrol beats, through writing up vicious beatings, through periodic bouts of violence, through cars and bodies damaged beyond easy recognition, through investigations that brought her into contact with the best and the worst of humanity, Lee had been OK. She had been, and she would be, so she told herself she was OK.

Now. OK. Yes. Now. Ahhh. O. K.

She looked again and liked what she saw much better than before. She looked like the person who had elicited whistles some days ago, who had attracted CC's attention, who liked herself.

Fortunately for Lee, maybe not for anyone else, a large cloud arrived and the glare of the day was gone for a long time. Heading off again, Lee arrived soon at the Café, only about ten minutes late. She walked into a nearly empty café, the only person in sight was a woman of about Lee's age. She rushed over, greeting Lee excitedly. At that moment, Lee could see Bob and CC talking in the kitchen. She was a bit annoyed that neither Bob nor CC seemed concerned by her lateness.

As CC opened the kitchen door, he called out, "Thanks, Janice."

"No problem, sir. Have a nice lunch," and she then walked out through the kitchen.

Almost simultaneously the phones of both of them buzzed and in unison they said "we have been informed you have arrived at the destination." Ah, she had been watched all along.

"Good morning, my bodyguards. Or should I say good afternoon. Not exactly the heart of lunch time."

"No, it's not," Bob said, "but notice"

A waiter was finishing pulling some blinds down on all the windows and a sign "Closed – reopen for dinner at 5pm" was placed behind the blinds on the door. The café was theirs alone, without prying eyes.

"Well done."

"We try," was CC's contribution.

"Here, sit at this corner table, not visible from the front in case anyone ignores the closed sign."

The wait staff retreated around the front welcome pedestal, leaving the three of them alone at the back table. CC was the first to speak.

"Good thing you didn't brush your teeth last night. We found the first inch or so of the paste in your tube was laced with a powerful, fast-acting sedative. I am not sure you would have had time to spit and rinse."

"Something like M99?" Lee asked.

"Not exactly. So, you are up on your sedatives, or you are up on your Dexter."

"Some of both. Had a case once where we needed to know."

"Anyway, you would have been out cold very quickly, allowing anyone wanting to get to you free access. But, here's the kicker. It was also laced with a slower acting truth-serum derivative. I think a controlled, soon-to-be-forgotten interrogation was to be the second act of the evening. The intruder wanted to know what you know."

"Great! Now, if only I knew what I am suspected of knowing. Before I forget, there is something I need to tell you about."

Lee then told CC and Bob about the other note waiting for her at the hotel. She also told them about the uneasy feeling she had while she was walking over to meet them.

Bob then joined in, "Maybe it will make you feel better to know that we are making some progress on our two paths of inquiry. However, before we get to that, I think we now know that the hotel is pretty worthless as a diversion, and a hotel is a hell of a place to try to keep under surveillance. We will make the room look like you are still there, messages will get picked up, room service might even be ordered and eaten, but just not with you in that room."

"Yes, let's focus on the apartment as where you will sleep, shower, etc. It is discreet, controllable," CC added.

"Now, on to what we have found," CC commanded, "and we have some new information. Most of the possible connections have turned up as dead ends. I looked at all kinds of espionage info, but everything I tried produced silence. But when we put out a query on String Theory, something interesting turned up. That phrase triggered a reference to some very recent chatter, creditable chatter, coming out of Russia. The most significant piece was a message about how 'the asset has been acquired.' That seems routine enough in the world of turning people, and even in the world of covert snatches, renditions as it were. But what triggered interest was what followed. 'Zamolodchikov again.'"

"Zammylachov?" Lee tried.

"Zamolodchikov," CC continued, "either of twin brothers from Russia who are String Theory pop heros.

OK, not exactly pop heros, but if physicists had pop culture status, either of these would have a nickname of 'Justin.'"

"Let me see if I have this right. The intercepted message talked about String Theory by mentioning a Russian past master of it and mentioned having possession of some asset?"

"Lee, you have it exactly. Someone, or someones, out there are letting others up their food chain know they have the person of interest connected to String Theory. Now, do we know of anyone like that who happens to be missing?"

"CC, I'll take an 'N' and solve the problem."

"Of course, this is not what we had hoped for. At the same time, it tells us that whatever they think you know, it is about the abduction."

"Are you sure Nottingham would not have gone willingly? Or that there is some coercion that might have made him go along?"

"We are working on that, but there is no indication that he had any love for the current Russian iteration of the Soviet enterprise, no indication of dissatisfaction with the US, no indication of any personal problems, no indication of family still over there, no deviant behavior to be covered-up, no indication of anything compromising. At this time, while we can't be absolutely certain and we will keep looking, we are working on the theory he was taken from the Conference."

"Sure fits."

"OK, Bob, it's your turn."

"So, if our boy's been nabbed, who did it? All we've got are the people on the trip and the people at the Conference. Let's start with the conference first. Nearly everyone there is so security cleared that it seems like an NSA convention. The only people not in that group were the few event staff and facility crew. Registration table person, nametag person, bathroom porter, A/V tech, facilities supervisor. We have checked all the security tapes and those are the only people ... and yes, we checked to make sure the tapes were not tampered with, and no, they are not tapes but solid state storage devices that means we have all kinds of embedded security data as well that would disclose tampering.

"Every person connected to the Conference has been cleared. So, we worked back from there. Our people, people on both the FBI and CIA sides, had him in their sights from the train platform to the Conference. That leaves us with the people on the train. We have looked at each and every person again, and we are at a loss there too. Once we eliminate the three suspicious characters – Lee, CC, and me – there is no one. Everyone accounted for."

Lee thumped her right fist onto the table, "Dead end! You have found a what, the acquisition by an outside force, but not a who. And I notice you are still missing any answer as to how."

"O, now it's 'you', not 'we'," chided CC.

"Hey, remember, I'm retired, and I'm the victim here. Don't see either of you with a bruise on the back of your head, or a home invaded, or a watch taken."

"So, I am going out on a limb here," Lee continued, "but I think the 'who' you need to look at more is ME! Now, before you object, hear me out. You two, and I when I am in a cooperative mood, are totally focused on Nottingham and Nottingham's disappearance. How about we re-focus on me and the various assaults on my simple, tourist, retired life. I sense there is something about me that is the key to all of this. Last night I was going to ask you two to help me with a little exercise, and then I pooped out, too tired for what I..."

Just then there was a knock on the front door glass.

Bob and CC suddenly became a pair of coordinated pantomime artists. Both of them signaled for silence. Bob pointed to the wait staff and then one of the more forward tables, made a circle and downward motion to tell them to sit there, and imitated downing a drink. The wait staff moved quickly and quietly into the positions Bob had directed.

At the same time, CC was motioning Lee and Bob toward the kitchen, in through the swinging door and out of view through the porthole window in the door.

All this occurred in about five seconds. As he entered the kitchen, CC nodded to the Maitre D' and then steadied the swinging door so it wasn't swinging at all.

As if calling from the back, the Maitre D' called out "Just a minute."

The Maitre D' did a quick scan of what he could see from the front of the dining room to make sure all looked right as he put ice teas in front of the wait staff now lounging at the front table.

Opening the door a crack, the Maitre D' said, "Yes, can I help you. We are closed until 5pm, and I would recommend a reservation if you want to dine with us any time after 7pm this evening. We're going to be full."

From outside a voice asked, "Are you Vegetarian or Vegetarian and Vegan?"

Inside the kitchen Lee, CC, and Bob all strained to hear what was being said. It was mainly a mumble of sound under the soft hum from the walk-in refrigerator.

"We serve both, and we can adjust any dish to match any dietary restrictions or desires."

"OK, that sounds good. Let me make a reservation then."

The Maitre D' opened the door and let the man in, motioning him over to the welcome stand with its reservation book. On the way over, he called to the wait staff, "Hey, break's over. Get back to the dish room and start the reset for dinner." The wait staff got up, carried their emptied glasses with them, and headed for the back, down the hall to the dish room.

"OK, sir, what time and how many?"

"8pm, for two of us. The name is Robinson. We are staying at the Radisson."

"Thank you, Mr. Robinson. 8pm, for two."

"Wonderful. O, any chance I could use your rest room?"

"Well, the staff has not cleaned it yet since the lunch rush, so please don't judge us. It's right back here."

The Maitre D' ushered the man to the hallway that led to the restrooms and beyond to the dish room. There was the sound of dishes being stacked and silver being sorted in the back.

"Thank you."

With the visitor closer to the kitchen door, the three listeners each suddenly perked up. CC popped over to the door window, got the attention of the Maitre D' and gestured for him to get the visitor talking some more.

About 2 minutes later the man emerged from the rest room. As he entered the main dining room the Maitre D' asked him, "Did you find everything OK?"

"If you consider that messy, I cannot think of having you in my home. See you tonight at 8pm. You have been most gracious."

The two of them walked together to the front door. The man offered his hand, and the Maitre D' shook it. Out the man went, and the door was shut and locked behind him.

Bob emerged first, again giving a gesture for silence. He slipped noiselessly back along the hallway and into the restroom. He was back in a moment and made a gesture like a small bug walking along his hand. The Maitre D' nodded. He yelled down the hallway, "Guys, come on. Don't take all day. Get a move on!" He then walked back there, made a similar bug gesture for the wait staff, and yelled at them more, including a little profanity. "Yes sir" "On it sir" came back. Then the wait staff went into the dining room and began the requested reset.

The Maitre D' waved to those in the kitchen to follow him. As they exited the kitchen, Lee looked over at the table where they had been sitting and saw the three half-empty glasses still on the table. "Damn," she thought, "it's always the little things." Following the Maitre D', they went to a side door, which opened into a stairwell that went up into the building above the restaurant. The Maitre D' wrote on a small slip of paper, "3rd Floor, down hall, cross over to other building, exit on back street." Thumbs up. OK sign. ASL for "Thank you." He quietly shut the door and the three were on their own.

The stairwell was not a public one, but a maintenance one: dark, worn, dirty, and perfect. It was evident from the dust it was rarely used. In silence they went up to the third floor, opened the stairwell door slowly and looking out saw a long corridor with various offices on either side. Midway down the hall another hall branched off to the right. The carpeted floor made their passage easier. At the end of the side corridor there was another exit door, the kind with the panic bar and a built in warning device when opened. Lee looked quizzically at the other two. CC nodded "yes." She tried the panic bar and it opened easily without noise AND without any bells or sirens sounding.

Out they went onto a roof shielded from street view by a very high cornice. About 40 feet away was the roof door of another building. Between where they were and that door one building ended and another began, with that high cornice continuing. "Thank goodness there is no gap," Lee thought. They made their way over the barrier and found the other door unlocked. That brought them down a stairway into another corridor with an elevator at the end. They summoned the elevator, a self-service one, and they took it to the ground floor. When the doors opened they found themselves in a lobby with a large plate glass wall looking out onto the street.

"We'll leave separately, about 5 minutes apart, and go our own ways. But as soon as we can, we will meet at Lee's place. Lee, go in the front way. We will come in the back. Lee, you be the last to leave here ... I can have someone here to tail you in about 5 minutes. So, between CC and the other agent you won't be alone. Ready?"

They both nodded.

Bob left, already on his cell phone.

About 4 minutes later CC got the text message that the other agent was in place. CC left, and headed a different direction. About 5 minutes later, Lee made her exit.

None of them experienced any strange activity on the trip to Lee's apartment. Lee's neck hairs behaved themselves too.

In about half an hour, the three were assembled in the sitting room where they had been about 12 hours earlier. Bob spoke first, "we swept the place again, and it's clean. And WOW!"

"Wow is right," Lee agreed.

"Did you hear him?" CC asked. "I think we all know who that was."

"Sure do. I'd know that Dutch accented English anywhere. But what was he doing there in that café?

Coincidence?" Bob wondered aloud.

"I think not!" Lee responded. "That was our fellow traveler from the Lake Shore. No doubt about it."

"What do you know about these?" Bob asked, as he reached into his pocket. "Found them in the trash in the bathroom." He pulled out a badly broken pair of sunglasses.

"Oh, No!" Lee gasped. "Those are mine. I lost them along the way to the restaurant, probably in the shop where I felt that anxious feeling. Shit, I loved those glasses."

"Forget the glasses. We were just delivered a message, a very threatening message. We can't prove he put them in there, but I called our people in the café and they weren't there when we came in. And by the way, in case you are wondering, that whole restaurant is our operation. All the staff work for us," Bob confirmed.

"Have to tell you as we were leaving, I noticed our drinks still sitting on the table where we had been. He would have walked right by and probably noticed. Hate it when the little things mess up all the precautions you took," was what Lee needed to add.

"Don't worry – I think we had already been made. Maybe not, but the sunglasses make me think so. We'll just have to go from here."

"Bob, let me check something out about the whole family. I have a hunch. I think we may have a little more information about 'who' is in our equation. But, the 'how' remains, and I am less sure now about the 'why.'"

"OK, CC, follow up on that idea."

"Lee, when we were so rudely interrupted, you were about to ask us to do something. Remember?"

"O, yes, I do. It is something I have wanted to try for several days. I have this nagging feeling that I know something that I am not remembering. The fact that someone else thinks I know something I can't remember is driving me nuts."

"But we questioned you over and over. You have told your story repeatedly, always the same core elements. What would be different?"

"It is a technique I developed as I moved up the ranks. It was not always easy to be a female cop, and a black female cop at that. I learned all the usual methods of interrogation, which work much of the time when you are trying to break down someone's defenses. But what if you are not trying to break something down? What if you are trying to build something up? Trying to put a thought, an impression, a memory together?

"This is what helped me move up the detective ranks. I was as good as anyone else at getting the perps to finally give it up, but I was way better at helping the victims and the witnesses to provide us with details they didn't know they knew."

"So, what do we do, and why?" Bob asked.

"OK, think about your usual interrogation mode. You want a stark room, bright lights, uncomfortable chair (at least for the person you are interviewing), and a series of fact-based questions. Who, what, when, where, how, and why? Sargent Friday – 'Just the facts, M'am' kind of thing.

"Turn it on its ear. Nearly dark room, subject comfortable, pace calm. Even invite them to close their eyes. Tell them to forget the facts, the details, but focus on both feelings and impressions. Don't worry about time sequence, or exact memories. All said in a calm voice."

"This begins to sound like some form of hypnosis."

"More like a form of relaxation exercise. When a person is in a fight or flight mode, when they are trying to defend themselves, every part of their being becomes defensive. What they have been hiding behind some inner door is now locked away beyond reach. Take away the need to defend. Become invitational rather than adversarial. And the interrogator gives the impression that she or he is giving control over to the subject. It is almost like saying 'You're in charge here, not me' which makes people feel safe."

"Don't know if I am up for this," CC admitted. "Not exactly my usual style."

"No problem. I wrote out some simple prompts for you, sentences for you to use if they make sense. And here's the really tough one, I suspect, for you two because you are, well, men who like to take charge. You want to talk very little, and when you do you want to talk gently and slowly. Things which have been kept hidden away don't come out if frightened. Ready?"

A pause followed, until CC said, very slowly and calmly, "Yes, I think so. Are you, Lee, ready to start?"

"Well done, CC!"

Lee then prepared the sitting room the way she wanted it. She closed the bedroom door. She went into the kitchen and filled the electric kettle. She took out an herbal tea bag from the cupboard and put it in a cup. When the water boiled, she poured some into the cup so it was about three quarters full. She moved one of the table lamps over into the corner on the floor and turned it on. She turned the overhead light out. She moved the lounge chair so sitting in it she would not see the lamp and so she would not be facing the two men on the couch but looking kind of parallel to them. She kicked off her shoes. She padded over to the kitchen, took out the tea bag and dropped it in the trash, and brought the steaming cup of tea in and placed it on the end table right by the lounge chair. She turned out the kitchen lights, took a long, deep breath, and sat down in the chair. She reached for the tea, blew across it, and took a sip. Then she leaned back in the chair so her gaze was toward the place where the wall met the ceiling. Several more deep breaths (thank goodness the two guys stayed quiet) and she let out a long sigh. She then lifted the index finger on her right hand.

CC and Bob looked at the notes they had been given.

"When I raise my finger, I am ready to begin."

"Ah," thought CC, "she is placing herself in charge. Pretty cool."

The two men silently read more of the prompts that Lee had supplied.

"Call me by first name. No 'Ms. Strangler' or 'Detective Comstock' shit."

"Bob, you will begin and you will continue until I mention CC."

"When I mention you, CC, in person, you will take over and continue until I mention Bob again, and so forth."

So, Bob began, reading slowly the first item on the page below a line that separated the instructions from the script.

"Lee, it was so good to meet you on that train from New York. Do you remember how you first met me that day?"

Lee then talked about casing the sleeping car, to find out who her fellow passengers were. About faking naiveté and confusion so she could more freely roam about. As she talked her narrative slowly began to change. In the beginning her voice and words seemed more a description of what had occurred, but gradually it moved from past tense and external to more present tense and internal.

"Here's Room 4 and there's an older man in it who looks like he's been blunting his feelings with a drink or two. He's reading and he's drinking. He's got a bottle of good Scotch out and I can smell it. He's reading a book. It's you Bob. You're drinking and reading. Or are you reading? You have the book opened to about midway, but I notice that the pages toward the front of the book don't look any different from the pages to the back of the book. I am a little suspicious because it looks like you haven't actually been reading it."

CC looked at Bob in the dim light, and Bob nodded, "Yes" and mouthed "wow."

"But, you are amiable looking, pretty harmless I would say. Probably a windbag, but a good-hearted one.

"I then look across the hall to Room 3, and it is empty. No one there yet. I know that they will also be traveling all the way to Chicago and their name is Carlisle and it is only one person.

"By then I am back to my own room and am looking across to that closed door on Room 1 and I am annoyed that I don't know who is inside that room, especially when it is so close to mine. I am very curious about who is in there. I know he is just one person, going to Chicago, named Alexander Nottingham. I am fussing in my mind about how I had hoped, actually fantasized, that the person in Room 1 would be alluring and inviting, but all I get is annoying and secretive. And I am thinking I know that name from someplace."

Even in the subtle light, CC notes that Lee's dark skin has taken on a slightly rosy overtone of blushing.

"Well, at least the train is leaving on time. I always love the dive through the darkness of the tunnel and then the sudden light as we emerge under the highway and begin to snake up the island until the river is in sight. But I am distracted as someone rushes by my room and mutters something about Room 3. I poke my head out to see who or what a Carlisle is, and all I get is a glimpse of one going into the room. Haven't got a clue about him."

Lee continued her narrative: Attendant Bruce, Room 1 wanting dinner in his room, dinner reservations.

"Wait, I am just thinking now that when I made that reservation anyone in an adjoining room would have heard and known which seating I was taking ... always those little things. When I was joined in the diner almost immediately by my neighbors, that might not have been mere coincidence. And then dinner. I meet Jean, and Uncle Bob (who is definitely carrying his Scotch ambiance with him), and this charming man in Room 4 who wants to be called CC. I was having the time of my life playing my assumed role, and they were all buying it. I ought to be on the stage."

At this point, CC took the cue, "So, you met me at dinner?"

"Yes, and you are on your way from New Jersey to O'Hare, to another convention or exhibit or something. And you have the most wonderful smile..."

The blushing undertone returned. Bob gave CC the eye, and winked.

"...and we four are really hitting it off."

Lee continued on about Albany, crossing the Hudson on the Livingston Avenue Bridge (Bob and CC were both amazed at the amount of train info she was bringing up, a far cry from the novice rider they were invited to experience back when it all happened), up West Albany hill, getting Bruce to make the bed down, picking up passengers in Schenectady.

"I am watching the Mohawk Valley glide by in the darkness. Little towns that once mattered somehow survive, a little worn for the trying. Utica with it's magnificent station. I decide it is time for sleep; it's been a long day. I close my window curtains and lie back down feeling the train slowing down. We are not near any station and I wonder why, and 'whoa," I am being tossed around as we change tracks. My hallway curtain is flapping a bit. I need to re-fasten it to its Velcro. What a minute. I can see HIM. Room 1 mystery man. He is brushing his teeth. He is real. He is human. Nothing special to see because all I can see is the reflection of his mouth and the toothbrush in the mirror above the sink. I feel relieved, like I can relax a bit. The castle wall of secrecy has been breached. And then sleep overcomes me. No, wait, it is not like that. There is a bump against the hallway wall just after that and I smell and hear you, Bob, careening back to your room."

Bob took up the lead, "so you slept through the night?"

"I did, it was wonderful. No, wait. I remember a dream. Or was it a dream. We are moving very fast, not stopped or stopping, but there is a noise, a noise that doesn't repeat. By the time I am half-awake, I know I heard it but I don't hear it. I know the noise. I know the noise. It is the sound of ... ah ... the door latch lock, the little lever, being shut on a room near me. On Room 1. The door to Room 1 was opened and then shut and locked again. And then I went back to sleep."

"And in the morning?"

"It is such a wonderfully lazy morning. Someone else will make me a delicious breakfast. But first I want a hot shower. It is such a wonderful shower as I speed along. Back in the room to get dressed and I can see him, or at least a part of him again, the man in Room 1. He is again brushing his teeth, and now he is lathering up to shave. Just like Dad did. Brush and soap. He is lathering his face. It is all I can see. He was brushing ... his teeth ... and now ... he is lathering to shave ... but something is wrong. It can't be. I am not remembering it right. Is it a trick of seeing something in a mirror?

Maybe. Let me think."

Lee, without moving her ceiling gaze, began making motions with her hands, motions of brushing her teeth. In a very excited tone, she erupted.

"It wasn't the same man! It isn' the same man. The man last night brushed his teeth right handed. But the man this morning is brushing his teeth left handed. He is using the shaving brush in his left hand. It's not the same man!"

With that Lee grabbed for her tea, now lukewarm, and took a long gulp.

"And then I sort of goaded the man in Room1 by asking if he wanted to go to breakfast, but he says 'I'm OK' ... no, that's not it ... 'I'm ... good' ... but wait. It's not the same accent as last night. Again, it's not the same man!"

CC and Bob stared at each other, and then back to Lee. They then looked at their crib sheets. Bob had nothing left to ask on his, but CC had one more question.

"Lee, we hear you. Just one more question, if you don't mind. Tell us about leaving the train."

"He was a different man, I tell you."

"Yes, I know. We can talk about that more in a few minutes. But put yourself back on that train. We all had breakfast, and then we arrived in Chicago (he was *ad libing* it now). What do you remember about the end of the trip?"

"I remember I really wanted to get a look at the man in Room 1. But it is all very confusing. Bob is inviting me to Milwaukee and CC is, well CC is CC, and I don't want to snub him, but the man in Room 1 makes his exit while I say 'goodbye', and all I see is his ... all I see is his back taking the turn in the hallway ... no, I see his back as he takes the corridor, and CC is being gallant and all, and I look down the hallway to where it bends around the bedrooms ... and I see, O MY GOD!"

"What is it?"

Lee's face had turned a washed out, ashy-black tone, and she seemed to be gasping for air. She was rubbing the back of her neck.

"The shoes, the god-damn shoes. He was wearing the same shoes as the man who was waiting for me by my door. The one who slammed my head and posed me for drunk."

"Are you sure?"

"Yes, I am fucking well sure! On the train, I now remember, it looked like the left shoe had been repaired because the heel was a slightly different shade of black than the upper, and there was a little bubble, like bead of glue, on the outside of that shoe. And I saw that same little bead on the shoe of the guy who hit me."

"Anything else?"

"Isn't that enough?"

12

STARTING OVER

Lee stayed seated, not talking for a long time. She seemed exhausted by the ordeal of remembering. She seemed bothered by it all.

CC tried to connect with her, "What's up?"

"I'm pissed, that's all. All of these details which could have helped us long ago. But, nooooo. The great detective retires."

"Lee, you are being too hard on yourself. Look at the facts. Two of the big guys, one FBI, one CIA, didn't figure any of it out either. Nothing we did pried any of that loose from your brain. You provided us with the technique, and a damn fine one it is. Your were like in a trance, right back there on the train."

"And, Lee, you saw and heard it all. The fact that you couldn't remember it before doesn't really matter. That you remembered now is what matters. Yes, we apparently have been spinning our wheels, but you set us straight."

"You think so?" Lee meekly asked.

"YES!" was their simultaneous response.

Lee smiled weakly, and then grinned. "Didn't do too badly, did I. Not bad for NYPD. Without me you would probably have cold cased this all before long."

She looked revived. She jumped up and headed for the kitchen. "I'm starved!"

A protein bar, some cheese, an apple, and some nuts later, Lee was bubbly.

"OK, what do we do now?"

"We start over," was the best CC could offer.

"Yes, let's begin again with our lists," Bob, in a revived mood himself, tried. "First list: what we now know."

They looked at Lee. "We know that Alexander Nottingham boarded the train in New York City, got into Room 1 on car 4911, virtually locked himself in until the train arrived in Chicago, when someone else got out of that room and left the train.

"That someone else then continued to pose as Nottingham while apparently the two top detective agencies in the world, the FBI and the CIA, tailed him to the University of Chicago and his intended Conference, where he was able to check in, seek a bathroom, and disappear.

"That this someone else would later appear in my doorway here in San Francisco and knock me over the head, planting evidence to make it look like someone else had done it.

"In the meantime, a Dutch family, here supposedly on vacation, have appeared on the train, and now not only in the Bay Area, but intersecting with our three lives on two occasions.

"Nottingham is still nowhere to be seen, and no one other than Nottingham is unaccounted for."

"Well done, Lee," was CC's assessment. "But I think you have missed a couple of key elements now revealed, or at least now revealed to be worthy of follow-up."

"Just a couple? I would hope my list missed many things, because each of those items would be a possible lead," retorted Lee. "So, Mister Sleuth, what are those elements?"

"Pipe or candlestick? Parlor or Library?" chuckled CC, "in this game neither of those represent important discoveries. But Colonel Mustard or Miss Scarlet, now there is the question. And the one that 'Clue' doesn't ever ask, 'espionage, blackmail, treason, or something else.' If we get to the why, the how and who will all fit, I am sure."

Bob jumped in, "Lee, your observing and remembering got us to maybe not know the complete 'who,' but it pointed us back with several assumptions clarified. And I need to remind you that CC and I were only 1 room away and we didn't see any of those details."

"That's true. I have been feeling worn out with the nagging feeling like I knew something, but I couldn't tell you what. It was wearing me down and out. I now see I was dreaming about it AND someone else was dreading what I might know. Of course, they had no way of knowing what and if I knew, but the fact that neither of your two agencies was hot on their trails must have given them the sense that I had not yet named names, nor figured it out."

"But now we know they know ... the note at the hotel, the visit to the café, the crumpled sunglasses."

CC, dutifully, brought them back to task, "So, here's the question I want to pose given all of this. Who on that train can't we account for? And I don't mean account for at the basic level. Who on that train didn't get off in Chicago with the rest of us? Whoever was then in Room 1 got off there. We three got off there. The Dutch family got off there. The fat couple. The mother with her child. Everyone got off there."

"Except one person," Bob quickly added.

"Yes," CC agreed, "except for the person who got on at Schenectady and off at Toledo. We did the usual check and found he did get off in Toledo, was scanned onto the bus at Toledo and apparently got off the bus in Ann Arbor. The driver is ready to verify that he got off in Ann Arbor. And later in the day, that man, Dr. Hildebrandt..."

"Did you say Dr. Hildebrandt?" Lee inquired.

"I did. Professor of International Relations at Union College in Schenectady. Specializes in international scientific treaties and patent protection. Why?"

"I don't know for sure, but we have a Doctor Hildebrandt who is the one other person we can't fully account for, only having some anecdotal evidence, and we have a Doctor Nottingham, who is the one person we can't find. Did anybody run any linkages between the two?

"No, or rather I should say, not yet. Let me get right on it." Bob ducked into the kitchen to phone.

CC used the break to put out another idea, " I continued to be troubled by the other continuity. You took the train out here, and we followed you. So we know why you are here. But why are the Dutch people here and still here. If their story was seeing America, why aren't they out seeing America. I want to follow up on them. As they say in our business, 'I know where they live.'"

"You are forgetting another person who is out here too, the person who left Room 1 in Chicago, disappeared on the south side of Chicago, and re-appeared in my doorway. I want to try to follow up on that, and I will need your help."

"Anything to help you, Lee. What do you need?"

"I need access, off the grid, to the people in your surveillance team out here. And I need some pictures."

"You got it."

"Here's the list of the people I need pictures of, formal shots OK, but informal even better." Lee handed CC the list. "And if you think some of Bob's people might also be of use, hook them up with me too."

"Right!"

Bob returned to announce that he had started the

inquiry into Hildebrandt, as deep as needed until there was nothing more to dig. CC filled Bob in on his concern about the Dutch family. Lee asked CC to show Bob the list of photos she wanted, and when Bob saw it he nodded and let out a whistle. "Not a fishing list I see. You have some sense of what you will be told, don't you?"

"I do," Lee responded, "but I was always taught to suspect wisely but accuse judiciously. I want all my ducks in a row before the shooting gallery opens."

"Lee, I will have one of my agents make sure you get those photos, properly labeled, in the next several hours, and that same agent will, when making contact, be able to assist you in making the other connections with the surveillance team. You might like to know that the agent who will contact you will be your old friend, Janice."

"Ah, Janice. I will be so nice to see her again."

"Bob, let all of us know what you find out about Hildebrandt. I have to go to Berkeley."

"CC, will this place be kept secure. Can we trust coming here as our rendezvous point?"

"Yes, front and back will be secure, and I am about to bring another agent in through the back, to spend a shift from hell sitting in the darkened bathroom lest anyone attempt another bugging or want to search or plant anything. With someone in here, the outside people can drop back just a little to minimize the chance of being made."

"Let's say we meet back here at 10pm"

"Fine by me."

"Me too"

And the three started over.

13

FAMILIAR FACES

Lee was the last one to leave the apartment. In the meantime, a wimpy looking guy came up the back stairs, showed an FBI badge and ID, and said "I guess I should ask to use the bathroom." Lee laughed and pointed to where it was. She added, "You will be relieved, so to speak, to know there is good cell reception in there."

"Thanks m'am. I appreciate that."

"No, thank you. I will be here until I hear from one of the other agents."

She stayed there for about an hour until her phone buzzed and a text message popped up. Lee was startled to see it identified the messenger as "Janice." "Not bad," she thought, "one of them found a way so the message from the agent looked like it was from someone in her phone from long ago."

The message simply said, "Great to hear from you and have I got some exciting news for you. Gotta chat soon."

Lee texted back, "LUV 2"

Almost immediately "How about now? Infusion Lounge, Ellis"

"CU"

Lee packed up her stuff, quietly waved goodbye to the agent who had taken up his post in the bathroom, his face lit by the screen light from his phone, and then went out the front door.

When Lee got to the Infusion Lounge she immediately saw it was the kind of place that matched her way of being anonymous. It was full of people, so she would just be another person in the crowd. It was lively and trendy. Nothing clandestine about it!!

She walked in and suddenly remembered that she had no clue what her old friend Janice looked like. Just then her phone buzzed and an SMS message popped up of a selfie from right there. Lee got her bearings, identified the backdrop, and yes, there was the person in the photo, waving to her. "Lee, Lee!"

"Janice," Lee said as she rushed over and hugged like a long-lost friend had been found. "It has been too long! Glad we could get time in our schedules."

Janice jumped right in, and it was soon evident that Janice had been well prepped on Lee's life. They really could talk like old friends, provided especially if Lee used her detective skills to focus the conversation back to Janice.

"O, by the way," Janice said in a suggestive voice. "I found these the other day, some photos of several of your old boy friends from back when."

"You didn't. O, No! The ghosts of boyfriends past."

"They're yours, if you want them."

"O, sure, why not. Might get a fantasy or two out of them."

"Thought you might like to know that the one on the top of the pile I saw here in San Francisco, out in the Mission, just the other night. He didn't see me, and I think I would like to keep it that way."

Lee smiled, knowing she had just completed one of her intended interviews with the agents without even having to ask. "Wow, thanks, now I can avoid him if I see him coming, so to speak."

The two broke down laughing like old friends. They were enjoying a slow drink together when Janice's phone rang. "O, damn, just got called back into work. Got to run. Look, if you get a chance, drop over to see me. I'll be at the City Art Gallery on Valencia. Might mean you would run into you know who, but I doubt it. He never was the art type."

"I will do that later. We can catch up more then."

Janice's phone rang again, "Running!"

Off Janice went. Lee opened the manila envelope, and looked inside. She saw the top photo and was not surprised. She casually looked at the other photos and they were exactly what she wanted. Now to connect with the other agents.

City Art Gallery took her back into her apartment's neighborhood. She wondered if this was a permanent front, or just a situational gathering place because it was close to the scene of the current action.

At least it was easy for her to find. She cased the place from the outside and saw that it was not a swank place, but more a gallery for the people. Good. She would not have to affect any airs. She went in and began to browse about. She was surprised because within a few minutes she had spotted several works she liked AND that she could afford. As she was looking at one abstract oil trying to decide if she liked it or not, a man looking at it beside her said "Oils are OK, but I prefer photos myself."

"O, do they have any photos in the exhibit right now?"

"I don't, but was told they did have some. Let me check."

She watched the man go up front and then Lee saw that he was speaking to Janice. Janice came running back with the man in tow. "Wow, you made it. This man, Harry was it?"

"Harold"

"Harold was asking if we had any photos being exhibited. We are about to open a small exhibit of some but the room is not yet set up to be opened. But for you, Lee, let me show them to you. And Harold, it is your lucky day. Come along too."

"Thank you."

Lee and Janice, arm in arm, joined at the hip like old friends, strode toward the back of the gallery with Harold following along. "Right here," Janice said, "and ushered them into a work room."

Not a picture on the walls! No photographs. Just a large worktable, some folding chairs, some file cabinets, and intense overhead lighting. Janice said loudly, "I think you will find these photos very interesting. I've got to go back up front, but take your time. And when you leave, please lock the door."

"Oh, Janice, you're a doll."

"Kiss Kiss"

"Kiss Kiss"

Harold just rolled his eyes. When Janice had left, they could hear her locking the door behind her. Harold then relaxed, and pulled out his ID for Lee. Lee reached for hers to reciprocate and realized once again what retirement meant. "Don't worry m'am. I know it's you. I have seen you many times in the last few days."

"I bet you have. And thank you. Now, I would like you to look at these four pictures and see if you recognize anyone."

Harold studied the pictures and then said, "yes, three of them. This one was around your neighborhood often, and this one was there a couple of times, and this one just twice. That last one stopped opposite your apartment for a long time about 2 days ago."

"Thanks, that's what I wanted to know."

"I'll send in someone else in about five minutes."

"Thanks, and again, thank you!"

"Just doing my job, M'am."

Lee stared at the photos and tried to place odds in her mind on what the other agents would tell her.

Over the next thirty minutes or so, three other

agents looked at the photos. All of them agreed with Harold. One of the persons pictured had been in the neighborhood often, another less often but there, and the third just a few times. The first person was always on the move, the second more at a distance and usually at night, while the last one lingered.

She thanked them all not only for this help but also for keeping her safe. The last one, a female agent, responded, "Just sorry we were not there to keep you from getting mugged. But we are there now. How is Andy holding up?"

"He seems to be having either adolescent or bladder problems. He is spending a lot of time in the bathroom," Lee joked.

"It is really a pleasure to serve someone who is in such danger and who still has a sense of humor."

Lee noted she had said "...who is in such danger..." Somehow she had not thought about that much when she was with CC and/or Bob, but sitting there alone it suddenly hit her. If someone had taken all the trouble to make Nottingham disappear, and then had mugged, bugged, and tried to drug her, maybe it was danger she was in, deeply in.

The agent, seeing a look of worry on Lee's face, quickly added, "and when you are ready to leave here, I can guarantee your safety right back to your front door. But I won't vouch for Andy. He might bore you to death."

"O, that type."

"By the book, no sense of humor, grim."

"OK, when I get back, I'll tell him I need to use the bathroom and see what he does because he probably has orders to stay in the bathroom."

"I like you!" With that, the agent offered her hand in what was more than just a polite handshake.

Lee waited about 5 minutes more, then turned out

the lights, left the room, and locked the door. She had tucked the photos into her handbag where no one could see them. She did not rush out of the Gallery, but stayed to see all the works displayed, making mental notes about two she really wanted to come back and consider for herself when all of this was over. She then played the part of old friend with Janice a bit more before leaving.

It was a relatively short walk home but she felt very safe. Not only did she know that agents were watching out for her, she also knew they were now more alerted to the faces of concern, and that three of those faces triggered awareness with all of them. If any of those three were to come into view, she was sure some kind of intervention would occur.

It was a pleasant evening, and she knew she was running early, so she stopped at a bodega and picked up some food and beverages. She would tempt Andy if she could. And she was already smiling at the thought of her demand to use the bathroom.

She unlocked the entry door, opened it, and started up the stairs. She was surprised to hear voices upstairs, a conversation. A raised voice and a much smaller responding one.

14

BACK EAST

Bob's job was probably the hardest of the three. His assignment meant he had to rely more on others than on himself. He needed to find out quickly all he could about Dr. Hildebrandt, his background, his connections, his habits, his whereabouts, and especially anything that might raise questions, flags, doubts.

He went back to the local office out of which he was working and started making calls. It would mean assembling a network of people: local police in Schenectady, Ann Arbor, and Chicago; other agencies in New York and San Francisco; and a few old friends not in any agency but in the know.

While he waited for responses, he laid out a large sheet of newsprint on the side table and used markers to draw the outline of the United States ("God, I wish I were better at art!") and then within that outline started using different colors to indicate who was known to be where. A red line went from New York to San Francisco. An orange one from Princeton along the red line until midway from New York to Chicago. A yellow line picked up from the orange line and into Chicago. A green one from Schenectady to Toledo, then to Ann Arbor. And then a green circle in San Francisco. A blue one arrived from the east into New York, and then followed the red line to San Francisco, with a side jog up to Napa and then back to just east of San Francisco.

Then he waited.

He waited for the phone calls to come in which he hoped would let him find out where all of these lines intersected other than the physical links he had drawn.

This much he knew. Something was missing from his map, and what was missing would help solve the case.

Schenectady called in first. Dr. Hildebrandt did indeed teach at Union, was a world-renowned authority (even the likes of the local cops knew about him), who was now on sabbatical. He had led off his six months of sabbatical with a conference in Ann Arbor at the University of Michigan, and now was scheduled to be somewhere in the west researching research. "Could you repeat that?"

"Yes, he is researching research, research methods that is. That is what the people at Union said."

"OK, thanks."

Next in was from within the CIA. Dr. Hildebrandt held a valid passport, used it frequently. Held a medium level security clearance. Was a known activist in several non-violent international peace movements.

"And his recent travels?" Bob asked.

"That's was what I thought," he said after hearing the response.

Bob had nothing yet to add to his map. And ironically, that was good.

There was lull in the action, and Bob took the break to close his eyes and power nap. He found himself quickly dreaming. He was back on the beat when he too was a cop. He was watching the classic three-card Monte game going on. He was in the lounge car of a train and someone was shuffling the cards. He could see the train, he could see the cards, but he could not see who was shuffling. He was just about to look up to see who it was when he was jarred awake by the phone ringing.

This time it was Chicago.

"Ann Arbor?"

"Sure about that?"

"OK, big thanks."

Now he had something to add to his map. He was looking for his green marker when the phone rang again. He was loving this. It was all coming together.

"Yep, yep, yep"

"Did you get the photos I faxed?"

"Really?"

"Both of them?"

"You're kidding me."

"Trifecta. Thanks!"

This was getting good. Now where did the green marker go, and the yellow one?

But the phone rang before he found them. This one was from Treasury.

"Did you run them?"

"And"

"And"

"You're making my day. I owe you more than one. Thanks."

As he had been talking, he had made a quick note. As soon as he hung up, he placed another call, a local call. He consulted his notes and asked for some help. It was brief and then he was back to his map, staring at it again.

In less than fifteen minutes the phone rang again.

"That was fast."

"Wait, let me get that down."

"Mucho Gracias"

With the phone down, he high-five'd an invisible person in a most non-Uncle-Bob fashion. "O, what I wouldn't give for a good Scotch right now."

His job may have been far from easy, but one of the perks of being on the job this long was that he had cultivated connections, both professional and personal, that were extensive, fast, and reliable. And in this case, these were self-proving: each of them verified a piece of what others said, except for one piece.

Now he was hoping that his newest connection would put that piece in place. He spotted the markers and began to update his map.

15

CC decided he would rather low tech it all. A walk over to BART, BART to Downtown Berkeley, walk up to the street where he had asked about the house where the Dutch family was staying. He didn't want to walk right in front of the house where he might be seen from inside. But he needed to know the number of the house.

He checked the block numbers again, and then walked up hill and back on College Avenue and onto campus.

A few minutes later a CC carrying several notebooks left campus on a run, flagged a passing cab, and gave an address in the block beyond the house that interested him. "Take College, and then turn right, I may see my friend walking back home. I've got something of hers she forgot."

The cabbie was more than willing when he saw the ten CC was offering up. Down College Avenue, a right turn, "please slow down, I don't want to miss her," ah, there was the house with its number prominent (probably as a result of it being a transient rental – can't have illegal renters wandering around).

"No, she must be home already. Just stop at the corner. Thanks."

"No problem," the driver said as he took the ten. "Change?"

"No, you've saved my neck."

"Anytime – take my card."

"Sure. Thanks"

And he darted out of the cab and further down the block. By the time he turned around the cab had headed back toward the campus.

Perfect!

Next he headed back into downtown Berkeley and into the first place he saw with a free WiFi sign. He wasn't going to be using the public WiFi (nasty, unsecured thing it is) but he wanted to be in a place where someone browsing on a smartphone would not look out of place.

Not out of place indeed. As he entered, not a single person looked up from some size of screen. They should call this place "Introvert Heaven" or "Loner Luau" or something like that.

He grabbed a beverage and found an isolated seat (although that seemed highly unnecessary). He Googled "short term rentals" in Berkeley. There were many, many listings. He then tried the search adding the address. Now there were five to choose from on various platforms, all with the same wording apparently. He chose Craig's List and up popped the listing, a photo matching the house, and lots of information about accommodations, prices, and reservations.

CC felt he had hit pay dirt. The pricing showed weekly and monthly prices, all set for 2, 4, or 6 people in the upper floor apartment. And the owner's contact information was shown.

CC drained his drink, threw the cup in recycling, and left.

Outside he found a secluded entryway of a closed shop. He first called and got an agent to come over and sit on the house. There were always FBI agents in Berkeley that could be assigned to the task. The campus and its activists had attracted the FBI ever since the Hoover days.

Then he called the owner. He properly identified himself as an FBI agent and said he would like to meet with the owner as soon as possible.

"O man, this is not about a code complaint, is it?"

"No, this has nothing to do with local government, and frankly I don't care if you are in compliance with local code or not. I am not referring anything to anybody, and if our meeting goes well, you will never hear from me again."

"OK. Want to meet me at my house?" He then gave the address of the very house.

"No, meet me in the front lobby of the YMCA Hotel downtown in an 15 minutes. Go to the desk and ask for me. I will have arranged for them to direct you to me."

"I'll be there."

"Thanks."

CC walked the several blocks to the Y, had a private conversation with the manager, and was offered a private room to meet in. About 10 minutes later a middle aged man was ushered in. CC showed his ID and invited the homeowner to sit down.

"So, you are the owner of the house?"

"Yes, I inherited it from my parents. Dad was a professor. They eventually subdivided the house so my wife and I could have the upstairs for us and our two kids. Dad passed first, and then Mom died about three years ago. We moved downstairs because the kids were grown and out of the house, and my wife had developed MS. It was easier for her to be down."

"Go on."

"But the MS got worse, and she had to stop working, and we decided we could rent out the upstairs. But we didn't want people all the time over us, so we decided on some shorter term rentals. We really like weekly, but we can deal with monthly."

"What about two weeks?"

"Funny you should mention that. We got one of those right now. A foreign couple, their kids, and their two uncles. Like peas in a pod, can't really tell them apart."

"The kids are twins?"

"No, the uncles."

"Really"

"So, what's this all about."

CC had to think quickly, although he had given it a short think-through while he had been waiting.

"This is part of a larger investigation into the patterns of short and long term housing, involving hotels, motels, AirBnB, Craig's List, Time Shares, Condos, and apartment rentals in relation to homeland security matters. Did you tell anyone you were coming here to see me?"

"No"

"Good. And I would ask that you keep both the fact and the nature of this conversation confidential. Now you may ask why? Because how rental properties are used by various groups, nationalities, and statuses is background information we need to have to predict and intercept future terrorists. Not your property, per se, but the overall pattern. In my report, your name and address will not be used. But the way your property is rented is important information. And the importance of this information could be compromised if the current, past, or future renters know we have asked."

"I understand."

"Now, tell me about your last four rentals, and the next four reservations you have."

CC tried to stay interested in the details he was provided about people he didn't care about. He had to periodically remember to make a follow-up question or comment. Then he read a summation of it all back to the owner so the present situation was minimized in the overall pattern.

CC then had several other questions about types of

payments, problems with payments, damage deposits and damages, and the like.

He then went back to one of the prior renters, the second oldest, and probed the hell out of them. He made sure to ascertain that there had been no contact with them since their departure about three month previous. Did he remember the bank they used? Did they have a car? And much more.

Finally CC brought it all to a close, and thank him for coming in, reminding him that discretion on this whole business was important. And then he drove the nail in.

"I told you this would not involve local authorities in any way. That will be true as long as both YOU and I keep this all confidential." Done!

"I understand. I want to keep everything as it is. Glad I could be of some help. Is there anything into the future I should be doing to keep everything secure."

"O. God," thought CC, "I never expected he would want to over cooperate."

"I think it would be best in the future if you would see ID's from everyone who will be staying in the apartment. Remember how much information you couldn't give me about that renter from several months ago. Probably good to see and photo copy their ID's."

"No problem. Can I go now?"

"Yes, and with the thanks of your government and your fellow Americans." CC almost felt like he should also salute.

"No, thank you! God Bless You!"

After the owner had left, CC put in a call to the agent sitting on the house.

"Any action?"

"Yes, somebody, a middle-aged man, left downstairs, and walked towards downtown. Then, a woman came to the downstairs door, and stepped out to get the mail, and had a hard time doing it, having to grab the handrails. Then, a woman with two young adolescent males, came walking up the street and went in the side door that looks like it leads upstairs. Since then, nothing. O, wait, the middle-aged man is returning and going in downstairs."

"Excellent. Now, keep on that house and give me a text with any more comings or goings. Call in a shift change as needed."

"Yes sir."

CC hung up and smiled.

If Lee and Bob had done as well, this re-start might be much more productive than the original go at it. And that was all because of Lee. She really was amazing, even as she put herself down for not remembering.

And then it struck CC. He wasn't thinking of her as a victim of a mugging, or as a former suspect. He was thinking of her as a colleague, not a retiree. They were a team. But no, that was not quite right. He may have been acting like she was a colleague, expecting results like she was a colleague, but when he thought of her he didn't think of her skills, he thought of her eyes, her smile, her shapely ... he was startled to suddenly see how much he both respected and desired her. He needed to remember this, because such blurring of lines can lead to mistakes.

But he was done for now.

He needed to hop on BART and get back to the apartment, hoping she would be there and not just Andy or Bob.

He walked over to the entrance and was lost in thought. Just in time he came back to the present and the location. Coming up the stairs into the underground concourse from the platform was Pier. CC quickly darted over to the farecard machines and began to purchase a card, fumbling for time. When he dared look, he could see the bottom half of the man going up the stairs to the street. That was close. He needed to be better on his guard.

The train was not crowded, he saw no one he knew, and before long he was taking the walk from the 16th Street Mission BART station. Just as he started out his phone buzzed. Text message "adult male entered upstairs door" CC texted back "OK – was he carrying anything?"

"Yes, some bags – looked like food." Good, explains why it took him that long to get home from the BART station.

As CC turned his duplicate key in the lower door lock, he listened. He heard three people talking, and one of them was Lee. He felt like he had come home.

16

PUTTING THE PUZZLE TOGETHER

It was a cozy little circle in the sitting room. When Bob came back, he had found Andy, but not Andy in the bathroom as he expected, but Andy just heading for the bathroom from the bedroom. Bob knew an agent had been assigned to be there, and knew the agent should be in the bathroom.

Bob already had out his shield and ID, holding it in front of him so the agent could see it as he entered. Halfway up the stairs he heard a loud noise, a pop. He called out, "CIA" When he topped the stairs and opened the stairway door he saw a person moving from the bedroom, Bob immediately drew down on him and shouted "FREEZE."

Andy froze.

While Andy was cooped up in the bathroom he had taken off his sport coat, so now his gun was visible, glaringly visible. Bob didn't know who it was, but he was armed, and he was in the wrong place at the wrong time.

"Ahhhhh, hhhhh," Andy tried, "Sir, may I show you my FBI identification?"

"I wish you would, because right now I am not sure which I want more, to shoot you as an intruder or shoot you because you are FBI."

As Andy fumbled around his body, he turned right red. "Sir, it is in my coat, which is in the bathroom. May I retrieve it?"

"Now here's what is going to happen. You will

slowly take your gun out of its holster, and holding it with your pinky, if you are strong enough to do that, place it on the floor. Then you will slowly kick it toward me. Then, you will turn around and place your hands on your head."

Andy complied. Within a few seconds Andy was handcuffed and then handcuffed to the radiator. Bob went into the bathroom, but first barked, "Don't move!" Andy didn't move.

When Bob returned he had Andy's ID in one hand and was holstering his gun with the other. "Son, I've got some yelling to do, and you are going to listen to it all. Of all the stupid things to do, be away from your post. You could have been blown away. I am dying to hear your excuse for the dereliction of duty."

"Sir, I had been in the bathroom when I heard two things – someone opening the front door and coming up the stairs and what sounded like gunfire out front. I went into the bedroom to see what was happening outside. You found me as I was going back to the bathroom."

"And did you see anything outside when you looked out the bedroom window?"

"Just some kids running down the block, throwing another lighted firecracker into a trash can. It must have been a dud, because it didn't explode." Just then they both heard another "pop" down the street. "Well, maybe not a dud."

"Did you at all think the sound might have been a test to see if anyone came to the window? How did you know that no one undesirable was watching the window. Did you think at all?" Bob was roaring.

"No, sir. I am sorry. I did not think."

At that moment, Lee arrived into the room. "Bob, what is happening."

"I am trying to convince this young agent that he is lucky I did not shoot him."

"I think he gets that. Now, get those cuffs off him

and let him have at least a shred of dignity. My God, don't you agency guys have any respect for each other?"

"Want to tell me about how your Queens precincts feel about suits from Manhattan coming in?"

"Point well taken. Now, let Andy get up."

Bob undid the cuffs, and even offered a hand up to the poor agent.

Andy collected his coat, and his ID, and his gun. "Am I done here?"

"Yes, you are, and thank you for keeping this place safe and sound," Lee offered.

"And for not getting shot. I do hate the paperwork," was Bob's semi-apology.

Andy was just about to the stairway door when CC entered. "Good to see you, sir," Andy said in welcoming him.

"Hope you have been a good boy."

Bob and Lee looked at each other, and a small laugh escaped Lee's lips.

"What?"

"Nothing."

"Don't tell me nothing."

"We'll tell you later. Andy kept the house safe, and I have lots to tell you."

"I suspect we all do and I want to sit down and hear it all," invited Bob.

Andy very formally shook each person's hand and took his leave.

Lee moved to the kitchen and asked the other two if they were still on duty.

"Lee, I went off the clock halfway back on BART," CC responded.

"And I, dear Lee, was off duty the moment that young man Andy left this apartment."

"Oh, Bob, don't be so hard on him. He was trying to keep us all safe."

"I know you are right, but it's always the little things that fuck you up. This time I hope I am wrong."

"Well," Lee said, "I know something that would be just right. Three Scotch on the rocks. Yes?"

Ice cubes dropped in three glasses, a bottle cork was pulled, amber liquid poured. Each of them, raising a now-filled glass, said nothing but just looked at each other, nodded, and then took a sip.

"Yes!"

After a long pause and a few more sips, CC said "You remembered, and made mine straight."

"Straight Pekoe, on the rocks, just for you."

"Thanks," and with that CC took charge.

"OK, here's how I see it. Bob, you took back east, where it all began, so we will begin with you. Then Lee, you checked out some key people right here. And then I'll be the closer, with some things I think will make sense after both of you have shared. Sound like a plan?"

Bob spoke up quickly, "Would have been my plan too. Here, look at this."

Bob took out and unfolded his map, and laid it on the coffee table. "Here are the various routes of key people of interest. Each color is a different person, solid for where we had originally accounted for them, dotted for where I have now found they have gone."

Lee let out a whistle. "OK, Bob, makes sense, but run through how you know it is true."

Bob then told his story, pointing to the map. CC, Lee, and he had traveled from New York to Chicago, as did the Dutch Family and several others. Lee and the Dutch family had then traveled on to San Francisco. Nottingham had traveled from New York to Toledo, where he got off and transferred to the bus to Ann Arbor posing as Dr. Hildebrandt.

"And you know this how?"

"The Ann Arbor Police interviewed the AMTRAK

bus driver. He told them they don't check ID's getting on the bus. Just scan the tickets since all the passengers came off the train where the ID's should have been checked already. But when he was shown the pictures of both Hildebrandt and Nottingham he picked out Nottingham as the person on the bus. How, you ask. A tiny mole on his face, just by his nose. Nottingham had sat on the aisle only two rows back and his face was in the aisle mirror the driver could see the whole way."

"So, Nottingham left the train at Toledo and he did so willingly, artfully in fact. He ends up in Ann Arbor."

Bob continued his narrative. He followed Hildebrandt's line now past Toledo to Chicago and down to the south side. "He was the person that our agents picked up at the end of the platform. The two look very much alike, so this was understandable as the crowd surged through. It was Hildebrandt that checked in at the Conference with the registration people who had never met Nottingham. From there he went into the bathroom, probably did a simple apparel change."

"But that puts Nottingham in Ann Arbor and Hildebrandt in Chicago, doesn't it?" asked Lee.

"Yes, it does. Now, follow this. Hildebrandt buys a cash ticket to travel on the AMTRAK evening train to Ann Arbor. An agent at Chicago remembered him because it is rare when someone that well dressed uses cash. In Ann Arbor he joins Nottingham at the motel; the motel confirms that Hildebrandt had reserved a room in Ann Arbor and a person presented himself as Hildebrandt for that single room. But the maid said all the towels had been used and she had the feeling that more than one person had been in the room overnight."

"It gets even better. On the afternoon after the Convocation, Hildebrandt alone rented a full size car for a three-week trip across the west, claiming it was part of his sabbatical. However, a service station clerk about a block from the car rental lot remembers the car because it stopped in the gas pump area and honked. He had gone over to it. The driver had said he was picking up a friend, and just then a man came along, threw a bag into the back, and got in. They left without buying gas or anything else.

"It seems that Hildebrandt had a debit card on an account in a somewhat obscure upstate New York bank, Ballston Spa. He never used it before, but on this trip he did. It took us a while to find the trail, but it led, in a very steady trip, through gas stations and convenience stores across the west, with one motel stop in Wells, Neveda. The trail does not end, but continues in the Bay Area. Most of the charges have been in Berkeley."

Bob now took out several markers and circled the Bay Area.

"Here we all are. You, CC, Me, Nottingham, Hildebrandt, and the Dutch family. Or at least it would seem that way. Nottingham has both disappeared and is now in hiding."

"Well done, Bob," was Lee's congratulation.

"Just one more thing, the rental car. I know right where it is. It is sitting in Berkeley, parked in a residential neighborhood not far from campus."

Lee picked up the thread. "And it fits with what I found out today. I had the FBI get me pictures of several key people. Nottingham, Hildebrandt, Pier, Mies. I showed them to the various agents who have been watching this apartment. They were pretty consistent. Hildebrandt and Pier have been around often. Mies was also recognized for a few visits, more recently, and then only to linger and look at this building. Pier seemed the most agitated, Hildebrandt more watchful, and Mies, how did the agents put it, she seemed 'thoughtful, almost sad.'"

"So, we have Hildebrandt here in San Francisco. And we have three of them interested in this place, probably interested in me. But no one had seen Nottingham. Sorry."

CC took up the tale now, "OK, Bob got them to San Francisco, Lee has them in San Francisco, and I will tell you where I think they are."

The other two looked amazed. "How?"

CC asked one question first. Was the rental car on a certain block on a certain street in Berkeley?

"Precisely. Amazing. But again, how?"

CC was in his element. Everything had gone his way.

"Well, my role was to follow up on the Dutch family. I decided to pursue them through their rental. I found out whose house contained the apartment, and was rewarded right away. The owners lived downstairs, are basically law-abiding citizen a little caught in the problems of life who are trying to make ends meet and hoping not to attract the authorities along the way by renting out the upper apartment.

"The owner was willing to meet with me off property and was most helpful. Seems the Dutch family rented the place off the Internet, paid cash, and, get this, are paying for six people to stay there. The four in their immediate family, and two uncles who look enough alike at a distance to be mistaken for twins. I thought we had found both Nottingham and Hildebrandt. That's why I thought you would find the rental car on that street or one near it.

"I have a watch on the house, and so far they have seen Pier return, and I almost ran into him in the BART station as he was heading home. Before that the mother and the two boys came back. My agent is now friendly with one of the neighbors, and I think it is one I spoke with also. She is like the maven of the block. She filled our man in on all the comings and goings. She doesn't like that the place is sometimes rented out, or she suspects it is rented out although the official story from the owners to the neighbors is that the sporadic strangers are all relatives of his wife's, coming to see and help her now her MS is getting bad.

"Anyway, our local source says the mother and the two boys leave almost every day about 10am and don't return until late afternoon or early evening. The father and one of the uncles go out both day and night for varying periods. But never the two uncles."

Lee gave CC a high five that connected with a resounding "CLAP!" "That does it, I think. We know where they are, how they got there. Nottingham is not really missing, just in hiding."

"Aren't you forgetting that they all seem to be here because you are here. That they have threatened you, hit you, tried to drug you, broke in here. This is not as simple as finding them, dropping by and saying, 'why Dr. Nottingham, so glad you are well and enjoying California.' Something else is going on and we need to find out what."

"I understand," Lee responded. "But what can we do? There is no sign that Nottingham was snatched, nor that he is being held against his will."

Bob began to answer, "What can we do? We can put some pressure on this family, this group, that is over in that apartment. We probably can't get to Nottingham, not yet. We have no probable cause of a crime. We did back when, but our own discoveries dissolve any semblance of a crime. Hildebrandt and the father seem to be the dominant figures in all of this. That leaves the wife. And lucky for us she is a foreign national. We can pick her up, just because. She is in this country by our leave."

"That's pretty hard hearted, Bob," CC said,

surprising even Lee with the passion in his voice. "Yes, legally we can do many things, but if the values we hold up as American values mean anything, then we apply them to all people."

"CC, you must be a real hit at the FBI office parties!" Bob countered.

"No, CC is right," Lee commented. "But it is one thing to treat a guest in our country like a criminal because we suspect something is not right and inviting a guest in our country to be helpful in their own well-being. Something tells me she is the weakest link, maybe the strongest link as a person which makes her the weakest link, in whatever is happening. Her seemingly emotional appearances outside this apartment lead me in that direction. And, yes, I am relying on a feeling but relying on feelings is what got me and kept me such a good detective. Boys, trust me on this one."

"OK, then what's the plan?" Bob asked.

Lee was slow in responding, but CC could see her pondering her plan and let the silence fill the time. Finally she said, "Tomorrow, when Mies is away from the house in a different part of the city, I need to go up to her and say I need to talk with her. I suspect she will be relieved for this to happen. She and her sons can then join us in some secure location. We can be alerted if any of the others from the house have left and might be shadowing her or us.

"Once we are in that secure location, you two will speak with her about the trip. She knows both of you from the train. You can begin by saying you were surprised when you saw her here in Berkeley. You were wondering why their plans seemed to change. In the meantime, I will stay with the boys. Remember, I am a retired cop with no real standing here. Whatever we talk about informs me but is not official to anyone. I am just keeping them safe while she talks with you. If I find out anything, I'll let you know. If you find out anything that might be illuminated by the boys, you let me know. How does that sound?"

"Sounds like a plan to me."

"Yep, same here."

17

CONVERSATIONAL DUTCH

The next morning rose foggy in San Francisco and bright and clear in Berkeley. CC, Bob, and Lee were in a small office in a tall office building just off Market Street. The front door said "Mission Hidalgo Educational Foundation." It was all a front. It was one of the several FBI covert meeting places scattered around the area. In this case, it was the most central.

"Everything in place?" Lee asked as she sipped some much desired coffee.

"As far as can be. Agents in place with hand-offs at various locations."

"Then we wait," Bob said with a resigned tone.

"And wait, and wait, and wait," CC quoted.

But they didn't have to wait long. CC's phone buzzed. He read the text message and then informed the others, "The three of them, Mies and the boys, are out of the house, and heading downtown."

"OK"

In a few minutes, the phone buzzed again. "They are on BART on a city bound train."

There was a longer delay, which they assumed was while the parties were making their way into San Francisco. Buzz. "Exiting at Embarcadero. No one else has left the house. No one has been following them."

"Other than us, you mean."

"Of course!" CC texted something and then told the others, "I have told agents that Lee will intercept and they will assist. And I suggest right now we turn off any sound or vibrate notification on messages, so we text without anyone hearing any notifications. And, Bob, could you turn off the sounds when you use your keyboard."

"Sure, just forgot to do it."

Lee left immediately, heading for the last reported location. After exiting BART, they were slowly walking up the Embarcadero. Lee found a car with an agent waiting to drive her. She directed him to a point several blocks ahead of the last location. Within minutes Lee was back on the sidewalk, walking toward the persons of interest. She was well aware she was being closely watched.

In about 5 minutes CC got a call. "The three of them are now in our possession. We should see them soon." CC talked some more and then told Bob, "Lee says she was right. That when she approached them, Mies greeted her directly and warmly. When Lee said that she would like to talk about things that have been happening, the response was immediate and positive. Lee said the woman looked around like she was looking to see if she was being followed, and then asked if Lee had anywhere safe to talk. The boys just stood by their mother and looked scared."

In about 15 minutes, there was a knock on the door. CC opened it and Lee greeted him with a smile and a wink. Behind her were the Dutch woman and the two boys. CC noted that there were no agents with Lee. Later Lee would tell him that she decided to keep it low key, so the four of them took the Muni, chatting about sights as they traveled.

As they all entered the room, no one seemed surprised to find CC and Bob there. It was as if they had known about the connections between Lee, CC, and Bob. Bob reminded himself to ask about that later.

"Mies would like to talk with you," Lee said to Bob and CC. "I promised to sit with the boys."

Lee was glad that Bob and CC were the only people evident; a bigger presence would probably have frightened her.

Lee took the boys out to the outer office and sat with them. She began with generic questions about their travels, slowly transitioning to their time in the San Francisco area. They loved the area of Sonoma and were upset that their father had gotten a phone call and suddenly said the weather made him feel sick.

That was when they came back to Berkeley. They thought that they would be staying in a motel and were looking forward to the pool. But their father had already rented an apartment. When they got there the boys thought they would each get a bedroom, but their mother had said no. The next day two men showed up who were said to be their uncles who had come to America years ago and who were working on a project.

While they were out each day, the uncles would work in the dining room with lots of papers scattered around. They weren't to touch any of it. Their father would make them leave the room whenever the uncles were working.

Had they been having a good time anyway? Yes, during the day when their mother took them on trips. Sometimes when they came home their father would be gone, and sometimes one of the uncles. The other uncle was always home.

When they would be trying to fall asleep, they would find it hard. They could hear their father and one of the uncles, the one who would go out, arguing. Then later they would hear their mother and father arguing.

Lee used the excuse of getting a drink of water to text CC: "Parents loudly argue at night; Pier and Hildebrandt argue too"

Meanwhile in the other room, Mies was telling CC and Bob about their trip. About how surprised she was to have a man from the train show up at the house they had rented. How Pier, her husband, seemed to know Hildebrandt but not the other man. How the boys had not seen Hildebrandt on the train because they had their beds made down and their room closed for the night just about when he would have been getting on the train.

It was then that Lee's message came in to CC. He saw it on his phone but didn't pick up the phone, acting like he had learned nothing. A few minutes later CC began to ask about her relationship with her husband. A long story started to flow out.

Mies and Pier had met at University. They had both been campus radicals, revolutionary anarchists in fact. But when Mies had become pregnant with the first of the boys, something changed for her. She started to think beyond her own anger at the system and think about making a better life, maybe not a perfect life for her child. The birth of her second son firmed up that resolve. But Pier had stayed idealistic. They fought about this often. He said she had sold out. She said he was more interested in tearing down than building up.

"So, that is what you have been arguing about lately?"

"Yes, and no."

"What do you mean?"

"Pier met Dr. Hildebrandt at a conference in Den Haag. They soon found that they both shared a great worry about what would happen in a post-cold-war world to keep a balance of power among nations.

"Pier thinks that if we can share technology around the world, no one nation can become dominant. Hildebrandt believes that the world was much safer when we had the US and the USSR, each trying to steal ideas from the other and both wanting no one else to join the club of elite nations. Hildebrandt said he knew about far too many secret meetings between all kinds of technical people on both sides during which there was an allocation of technology so that neither could beat the other, and no one else could beat either of them.

"But Pier, he felt that it was safer to have lots of people sharing the technology so everyone was equal."

"It was about a year ago that Hildebrandt wrote to Pier, and said he had been thinking about their disagreement, and maybe Pier was right. Then about six months ago he called to tell Pier that he now knew Pier was right, and that a friend of his here in the States, a scientist, with lots of innovative ideas, shared this view.

"Before long, the three of them were communicating by email. Pier announced that we were going to America for a long trip. I had always wanted to see the US, so I was happy. But he said there were some rules. On the train, we were not to get very friendly with any of the men passengers. He said he would say why later. He never did say.

"But when I saw who came to our apartment here, I knew why. These were his friends. And they were plotting something. The scientist would work almost all day, and he was not to go out or even near the windows. Hildebrandt said the government was after him because they didn't want him openly sharing his ideas.

"Then Hildebrandt began to change what he was saying. Hildebrandt began to speak about balancing the power in the world by re-creating a situation of two great powers. Pier would argue with him. Hildebrandt said the government would do anything to shut them all down, and the scientist, he was called Alex, Alex would get arrested for helping other countries, he would go to jail, and only America would have the information. That would be the worst outcome.

"Pier would yell at him to get real, and remember bigger ideas. Hildebrandt continued to change, saying he needed to do whatever he needed to do to protect Alex, and himself.

"Later in the night I would ask Pier, 'why doesn't Hildebrandt want to protect us?' and we would fight about it. Pier said he didn't like the idea of violence and was trying to talk Hildebrandt out it. Then one night, Hildebrandt came home and said he had taken care of the biggest government threat. He had a wild look in his eyes. He also smelled like you." At that she pointed to Bob.

Bob used that opening to ask, "What is the scientist, Alex, doing?"

"He's putting down many formulas, and he is using them to show how things could be made, or codes could be created. Yesterday he said he was almost finished. Pier and Hildebrandt got into a fight. Hildebrandt tried to gather up many of the papers, and Pier had to stop him. Finally they agreed that Alex would keep them for now. Last night I told Pier that he should not leave the house because who knew what would happen when Hildebrandt and Alex were home alone."

"Mies, are you worried?"

"Yes, Hildebrandt keeps getting angrier and angrier, and more violent in his talk. I worry about what my boys see and hear."

"How about if this afternoon we treated you all to a nice boat cruise around the whole bay, including lunch, while we see what we can do?"

"That would be wonderful. But will you arrest my Pier? "

"No, not unless he does something illegal between now and when we get over there, or when we get over there. No law has been broken by him. But Hildebrandt is a suspect in a mugging."

"Mugging?"

"He beat someone up. In fact, he beat Lee, the

woman from the train, the one with you boys right now."

"Ooooo," Mies moaned. "I was afraid of that. He has said some awful things about her. That she had to be stopped. That she knew things that would ruin it all. That he would frighten her away. I was worried for her. I sent Pier over to watch her whenever Hildebrandt was out. I would always give him a grocery list so when he came home he could say he was out shopping."

"Only your husband?"

"No, two times I went to the house where she was. I liked her on the train. Hildrebrandt said she was Police, that she lied about herself, her name, and all. But she was kind to us. So I thought about going over to talk with her, to let her know about Hildebrandt. I almost got up the courage to walk over to the ring the bell, but then I saw Hildebrandt coming from up the hill and I went around the corner. I never went back. So today, when she came up to me, it was very good."

"She said you would feel that way. Now, how about we get those boys of yours and take you down to the Ferry Terminal and that boat tour."

"We would like that. Thank you. And please, don't hurt anybody."

"We don't intend to."

CC and Bob stood up, a signal to Mies to do the same. Bob opened the door to the outside office, and when Mies saw Lee, she ran to her, tears flowing, hugging her. "I'm sorry. I'm sorry. It was not family."

"I know. I know. These wonderful young men," the two stood taller at being called men instead of boys, "have shared how much you are worried about what is going on, and they think you are trying to keep their father from getting hurt."

"They're right," CC said. "Your mother is helping us to make sure everyone is safe, that no one gets hurt."

"Now, we need you all to be out of the way for a time while we go make them all safe. How about a tour of the Bay, including lunch?"

"Alcatraz?"

"Of course."

"Wow, we need to Tweet all our friends."

"No, no Twitter, or Facebook, or anything else about where you are until we tell you."

"It's a secret mission?"

"Sort of."

"No problem, mon" the younger one said in a very poor Jamaican accent.

Mies tussled his hair and said, "Maybe you should stick to Dutch."

Mies and her two sons were introduced to two other agents who were charged with getting them onto the tour boat, staying with them for the tour, and then bringing them back to the office afterwards. The agents looked pleased for the assignment, especially Andy who was beginning to worry he would be on bathroom detail again.

After the others had left, Lee asked, "So, what do we do now?"

18

IT'S ALWAYS THE LITTLE THINGS, AGAIN

" **D**on't know what YOU are going to do, but Bob and I have business in Berkeley."

"What?"

"Look, Lee, you are a retired New York cop, without any standing here."

"That reality was pretty useful this morning."

"Yes, but now we get to some work that has to be by the book, legal. You'll have to sit it out. Please, Lee, go back to your apartment, and wait there. It will be my pleasure to personally come see you there and tell you how your help meant we could wrap this up in an efficient, peaceful manner. You could then offer me a nice beverage, because by then I would be off duty."

"O, you sure do know how to sweet-talk a cop."

"How about sweet talking a lady?"

"That too!"

"OK, I'll play along. Maybe I can finally get onto the vacation I promised myself back at Penn Station. Ciao, Ciao!"

With that, Lee made the most dramatic exit she could, pecking Bob and CC on the cheek, twirling around between the two of them, shouting "Ole," and then tap-dancing her way out of the room.

For the first time in a long time Bob and CC were speechless until they both broke into laughter. "She's really is something."

"Yes," CC concurred, "something and something special."

"Do I hear something more?"

"A trained agent like you should be able to tell!"

"Maybe after today's activities I will start an investigation."

"You do that. I plan to start my own investigation into this when this case is done."

The two of them turned to some paperwork. CC hooked up with his various eyes on the ground. No one else had left the apartment in Berkeley. Nothing unusual seemed to be happening.

"Bob," CC finally said, "I think it is time to get over to Berkeley. Now we know where all our subjects are, it is time to act."

"Agreed. Let's roll."

"But first, I need to set something up." CC was immediately on the phone to the homeowner in Berkeley. He explained there was a real need for the homeowner to get out of the house; that he was not to talk to anyone other than his wife about this.

"But, what about my wife. She's having a really bad day."

"Will she play along with an assurance this is important?"

"Yes, I am sure she will."

"OK, here is what you will do. In about 10 minutes you are going to call 9-1-1, and request an ambulance to your house. They will come in, put your wife on a stretcher and take her out and away. You will grab a few things, lock your part of the house, and rush out to the ambulance and ride with her. The ambulance will not take you to any hospital, but to a safe place about a mile away. In about an hour, we should be able to bring you home. You will have our deep appreciation. And I promise to come over and explain all of this to you. And I double promise no local official is going to get involved in the upstairs rental."

"Ready. 10 minutes. See you later."

"Thanks. Thank you!"

CC immediately dialed another number, told the details of what he wanted arranged. Hanging up he looked at Bob. "In 30 to 40 minutes, we will be ready to move in on that house. So, we better get moving. I need to send a few texts, but I can do that as we drive."

The texts were to the agents sitting on the house. They were informed of the ambulance coming soon and told to react to such an event in an appropriate manner – join any crowd that forms, don't just sit in your cars.

Bob and CC in one car, and four other agents in another car, headed out. They were about halfway across the Bay Bridge when the first text came in – "Ambulance here, wife moaning loudly." Then a second, "At the apartment. Keep me posted." And a third "Subject Lee now inside apartment."

Off the bridge, up past IKEA, left at the split, into Berkeley, onto the local streets. The two cars pulled up a block short of the house. CC did another check. "Anyone in or out of the house?"

Three different responses, all the same: "No, only the first floor couple out."

CC and Bob each informed their agents on the ground that the six of them were coming including descriptions. The orders were given that as soon as the six made entry into the upstairs door, the other agents were to converge and protect the perimeter.

The entry agents were all reminded about putting their badges in plain sight just before entry, to call out their agency name, and move quickly.

CC and Bob were each leading the two groups of three up the street toward the target block when CC stopped in his tracks. "Wait up. Just need to double check the status." He texted again and again received verification that two of the three men from the house had been seen go in and not leave while the third one, the one never seen, had neither gone in or out.

"What's up?" Bob asked.

"Don't know. Funny feeling. Like there is something, some little thing we are overlooking."

"Want us to stop?"

"No, let's go. Bob, you and your people go in first. We'll follow."

19

HAIR ON THE BACK OF ONE'S NECK

Back in the apartment, Lee was relaxing, maybe relaxing for the first time in a long time. The "bad guys" were all located and probably by now had been taken into custody.

Nottingham would have explaining to do. Pier would probably be asked to leave the country. Hildebrandt would be arrested on multiple charges.

And CC would need to tell her over and over again how much help she had been.

It was the first time she felt comfortable with the bedroom drapes opened wide, and the nightlights in the neighborhood looked festive. But she was having a hard time keeping her eyes open. She thought about how little sleep she had gotten in the last week. She had been running on adrenaline much of the time, that and coffee, and ... she had to admit having CC around had kept her alert too.

She started day-dreaming, but that slipped rather quickly into an actual dream. She was back on the train, in Room 2, and CC was in Room 1. He was looking over toward her. He was smiling and saying "Hi." In the way that dreams proceed, in an instant he and she were in Room 2, looking at each other from the facing seats. Then she suddenly was lying with her head on some pillows, and ....

"What was that sound?"

Lee awoke with a start. There was a sound.

It was a door opening. But not the front door. It was the back door. Was it CC coming to deliver the full follow up? Yes, that was probably it. But he said he would either text or call. Oh, it had to be he. The back door was still being watched by an agent. Or was it?

A voice called out, "Detective Comstock, it's Agent Myers. The back door was ajar and I wanted to make sure you were OK."

"I'm fine. Thanks for checking."

"That's good."

She heard a few footfalls on the stairs and the back door closing and locking. How did the back door get ajar, she wondered. But there was something else that was bothering her, and that something else had those neck hairs doing a full conga line.

"That's good," echoed in her mind.

Then she had it: "I'm good." Said behind the closed door of Room 1 way back when they were crossing Indiana. She was going up to breakfast and decided to goad the mystery person in Room 1 a bit. "How about some breakfast?"

The person she had assumed was Nottingham had said, "I'm good." But now she knew the person in Room 1 at that point had been Hildebrandt, and that was the voice from the stairs. She had not seen the agent, only heard him. It was enough to identify him in her mind.

Now she was remembering that the evidence all pointed to Hildebrandt as the person who had mugged her in her doorway. It was Hildebrandt who left her dead rodents as warnings. It was Hildebrandt who had planted the bug. It was Hildebrandt who had put the sedative in her toothpaste.

It was Hildebrandt who was now standing in the stairway door frame, looking right at her.

"Don't reach for that phone. Don't make any loud noises. We need to have a long talk before I decide what I am going to do with you."

"How did you get in here? The back door should have been watched."

"It was until that woman got the same treatment you got, only harder. And I didn't put the sedative in any toothpaste, I put it in her mouth. She will be out for a long time."

"But, how can you not be in the house in Berkeley? No one saw you leave."

"Yours is not the only house with a little known back door. When that ambulance came to put the old lady in the hospital, I used the disturbance as a good occasion. I didn't know if we were being watched, but I doubted anyone would be on the next street over."

"What if I were to tell you that the whole scheme is over. That agents from the FBI and the CIA are at this very moment raiding that apartment. They will have your accomplices, and Dr. Nottingham's work."

"No, I have it all right here." Hildebrandt tapped a black backpack. And it is all going where It will do some good, matching America's arrogance with an equally powerful nation that can do something with all of this. You can have Nottingham, I have his ideas."

Lee was getting more worried. In the last speech, Hildebrandt's tone had changed. He sounded very angry, very passionate. Passionate people often end up doing very irrational things, and she didn't want to be the object of his irrationality.

"Dr. Hildebrandt," she began.

"I see you know who I am, which tells me you know much more than you let on. I never really met you on the train, but the one thing Nottingham told me was to watch out for the woman in Room 2. As time went on, I could see why. Now I know for sure. I should have finished you back when I had that chance. Another tourist murder in The Mission. Nothing to look at here, just keep moving. At that point, I don't think you had made contact out here with either of those Fed clowns."

A chill went down Lee's backbone.

"Dr. Hildebrandt, you had the chance to completely silence me but you didn't. Now, while I can still talk, I want to compliment you on your plan. You should know that if it hadn't been for my cop instincts, you would have gotten away with it."

Hildebrandt seemed to soften a bit under Lee's flattery.

She went on, "In fact, it was the littlest of things that gave you away."

She kept telling herself that as long as she kept him talking, he was not going to act.

"It's always the little things."

"Like what?"

"OK, you have been working with Dr. Nottingham for several days. What hand does he write with?"

"His right."

"And you?"

"Oh, dammit!"

"You worked out all the big details, but it will always be the smallest ones that get in the way."

"And you must really like those shoes. I see you have them on tonight. You had them on when you left the train. And you had them on when you waited in my doorway. Again, a simple change of shoes would have left me with nothing important to remember."

"But in the end, even with my slip-ups, my little mistakes, I have the data, and it will be overseas in a matter of hours, and by this time tomorrow the balance of power in the world will be closer to even, and the world will be safer. You can remember all you want, but in the end, I win ... and you lose!"

As Hildebrandt said that last phrase, his voice raised to a fever pitch, he drew a small gun from his waist band just out of sight, hidden behind his coat panel.

"Yes, they will know who did it. But by then I'll be in the protection of another great nation and I will teach them to ignore patents, which are just the capitalist imperialism of the information age. Nottingham's ideas, based on String Theory, will help them build security measures behind which they can proceed unseen, just as this country has done. You'll be gone, but I'll be gone too. And that CC and that Bob can kiss the memory of my ass. You see, once you were insignificant, then you became important, and now you are, just expendable. And in the end, no one will care."

"I will!"

CC now stood in the frame of the stairway door, his gun drawn and pointed right at Hildebrandt.

"William Hildebrandt, you are under arrest, on charges of assault and attempted murder, assault on a Federal Officer, and I am sure there are other charges to come."

"Don't I get my Miranda Rights?"

"Not until you put your gun down."

At that moment, Hildebrandt began to lower his gun but suddenly lunged to his right and raised the gun again, pointing right at Lee.

A shot rang out. And another. The room filled with gunsmoke.

Lee, as an experienced cop, as soon as she saw Hildebrandt shift suddenly, shifted in the opposite direction, making herself as small as possible, and trying to get behind the lounge chair. The back of her neck hit the edge of the end table, and she was suddenly unconscious.

When she awoke, she was on the floor, surrounded by several people. "Where's CC?" was the first thing she asked.

"He's on the phone ordering three ambulances, one for you and one for our agent out back, and one for our suspect."

At that moment CC came into view. He knelt beside Lee and asked how she was feeling. "Better now you are here. Where am I hit?"

"Hit. You mean shot?" CC pointed to a big hole in the plaster wall behind where she had been standing while she had been talking with Hildebrandt. "Your move dodged that bullet by several feet."

"And Hildebrandt?"

"He's going to need a knee replacement, but he will survive to answer for what he has done."

"What about everyone else?"

"Mies and the boys had a great afternoon, and Mies is very relieved that it is all over. Pier is being cooperative, and is regretting ever believing Hildebrandt. He feels like he was duped. Nottingham is also glad it is over. Somewhere along the way he began to suspect that Hildebrandt had changed allegiance and philosophy, so most of his notes are elaborate concoctions. He says it is a good thing String Theory is so misunderstood because it made it easier for him to pass gibberish off as important ideas."

"How about the agent out back?"

"She will have an egg on her neck about the size of yours, and we are working on flushing the sedative out of her system. She will be fine. She sends her apology."

"Tell her none is needed."

"Want to share the ambulance with her? Dispatch says the third bus will take a long time to get here."

"Sure, misery loves company."

20

It was ten days later when Lee Strangler boarded the eastbound Lake Shore Limited in Chicago. After a short hospital stay and a few things needing cleaning up, she was cleared to leave. In that time she saw CC only once. He was busy. She knew all about the reports that would have to be written, made more complex by inter-agency relations.

Her presence in all of this also complicated the reports. She was central in a way, but was not officially there at all. CC had come by to get her signature on a several depositions. She had thought she might see him on the morning she left Emeryville heading south to Los Angeles. Three days in LA was more than enough for her. From there she got on train 4, the Chief, and rode the old Sante Fe line back to Chicago.

It was a miserable trip. Or rather, she had been miserable on the trip. She felt lonely in a way she had never felt before. She felt aimless in a way she had never felt before. Was it retirement, or something else. She had her whole future in front of her, without obligation or restriction, and all it did was feel empty.

Her train arrived a few minutes early, and so she had about 6 hours to kill.

She retraced some of her prior steps, finding her bench by the lake, She found it hard to believe all that had happened between her first time there and now. She wished she had someone to tell about it all. She found a great steak place in the loop and was thoroughly enjoying some fine cheesecake after a magnificent porterhouse when she realized she had only half an hour to get back to Union Station, grab her bag from storage, and get aboard.

The train was already loading minutes before she had her bag. Walking down the platform, she liked that this time her car would be a short walk. Yes, there it was. And she wasn't play-acting anymore. An attendant asked where she was going, "I'm in the eleven car," was her answer. Her car attendant asked if she knew where her room was, and she said "I could probably tell you things about that room that even you don't know."

"Like what?"

Looking at the permanent number of the Viewliner Sleeper, she was certain. "I'd say that in my room, on the wastebasket, there will be a small piece of duct tape, and the initials LS. Tell you what, why don't you take my bag to my room, take a look, and see if I'm right."

The attendant took her bag, went up the stairs into the car. In about 2 minutes he was back. "Well, I'll be damned. Sure enough, it's there."

"I know my trains. My father was a porter, then a car attendant."

The attendant looked at his manifest, and then whistled. "You're Strangler's daughter. Why, I remember you from back when I was starting, and he was so proud of you. You're a cop, Right?"

"Retired cop. Done with the job."

"I'm heading for retirement too, only have two round trips and I am done. I know what I am looking forward to, so, Ms. Strangler, I'll keep the cops and foamers away from you."

"Thank you."

Lee walked up the trap stairs and turned right into the car. Past the bedrooms, around the corner, and there was her room, Room 2.

And across the hall from her, Room 1, the door was already closed, the curtains already drawn.

"O, no," she thought, "it all starts again." But this time she didn't check the manifest. She just settled in.

Right at 9:30pm, the train made those sounds that trains make in getting ready to leave. Brakes released, traps shut, "All Aboard" echoing. With a slight lurch she began the last leg of her trip back home and into her future.

Past the 21st Street bridge and the train started to pick up speed. Just then the door in Room 1 rolled open, but the curtains stayed closed. In a minute or two she began to pick up the faint scent of Scotch. A hand reached through the curtains with a wonderful Scotch on the rocks, offering it to her.

She knew that hand. And that voice.

"Misery loves company."

When CC drew back his hallway curtain, Lee felt happier than she thought she ever had. Not only was CC there, he had gone out of his way for her. But, she had to make sure.

"This is not another assignment, is it?"

"I hope that isn't Scotch in your glass.

"I hope that isn't Scotch in your glass."

"Oh, but it is...finest Scotch tea, that is." And by the way, the Scotch is courtesy of Uncle Bob. He instructed me as to the precise single malt to get, and told me to make sure you enjoy it because you surely earned it."

"Then, what shall we drink to? Health, happiness, world peace?" Lee asked.

"How about 'to us'!"

Lee felt a small tear starting down her cheek.

"Yes, 'to us!'"

About the Author

Randy Becker is a retired Unitarian Universalist Minister who now calls himself a spiritual activist and troublemaker. But before all that he was a railroad engineer and a research physicist. He divides his time between Key West, Conch Republic, Litchfield Township, NY, and as much traveling as he can afford (usually by rail). Maybe the next time you are traveling by train he will be watching your every move and you could end up in one of his mysteries.

ABSOLUTELY AMA⚡ING eBOOKS

AbsolutelyAmazingEbooks.com

or AA-eBooks.com

www.ingramcontent.com/pod-product-compliance
Lightning Source LLC
Chambersburg PA
CBHW050400030726
47503CB00006B/1954